The Most Important Thing

M. E. Matthews

The Most Important Thing

Copyright © 2016 M. E. Matthews

Published by: DeLorge Publishing

ISBN: 0692637575
ISBN-13: 978-0692637579

FOR DAVID

1

The journey of life is a long drive. The destination at the beginning

of one's journey seems so far away that it feels completely

unattainable. Then on a rather ordinary day, the end looms over the

horizon, every step a moment closer to the inevitable. Melanie's

life consisted of To-Do lists, goals, desires, and accomplishments.

Everything she set out to do, she did, one way or the other. This

evening was no exception. She stood there at the sink, scrubbing

away at the white casserole pan unwilling to let the baked on

cheese get the best of her.

She had started this meal early in the day, planned a romantic

dinner just for her and her husband, Jeff. They had an overnight to

themselves; their girls were away and the youngest fast asleep. She

hoped to make the most of the occasion and perhaps breathe some

life back into their lackluster relationship. It had been too long since she felt more than just a quick caress or a kiss in passing. Most of the dinner consisted of him responding to emails on his phone than in conversation. Melanie silently conceded that she had lost this battle but not the war.

"Why don't you just throw the pan away? It's not like you can't afford another one," Jeff said as he passed by her refilling his wine glass before returning to the living room to watch TV.

"It's easy to give up but I've had this pan for ten years, and I know it will come out," she said with a sideways smile before returning to her task. Like most things in life, all that pan needed, all their marriage needed was a little work. She would put in enough effort for the both of them she as always did.

Melanie continued scrubbing the pan, if she gave up on the simple things how could she expect to tackle the larger problems in her life. The issues she struggled to deal with and never spoke of if she could help it. Eventually, after a few more rinses and a lot more hard work the pan sparkled like new again. Melanie held it up, proud of herself before sitting it on the dish rack to dry. Grabbing her cup of tea, she settled on the couch next to Jeff; everything would be perfectly fine she thought smiling to herself.

Everything was perfectly fine until it wasn't. The house was dark; the only illumination came from the television that was now playing an old *Leave It to Beaver* episode. The DVR had cut off a long time ago reverting to TV Land. Jeff arose with a start and then noticed the house was silent. He was accustomed to falling asleep watching TV and life just going on around him. Melanie would continue her chores and take care of the kids while he got some much-needed rest. It wasn't that his job was hard, just for some reason all his good thoughts, the ones he won all those awards for, came in the wee hours of the morning. Most nights he stayed up pouring over his accounts long after Melanie fell asleep.

Tonight, it was too quiet. Jeff quickly got up off the couch and looked at the clock, 11:05 pm. Melanie would be asleep by now, but it was odd that when she came home, she didn't wake him. He walked up the stairs from the family room and down the hall to their master suite. The bed was empty, undisturbed from this morning when she remade it. He walked back in the other direction towards Jack's nursery, he laid there sleeping and the girls' rooms were empty as expected. Sara's room, a Pepto pink, affectionately called the pink nightmare by Jenny who preferred navy blue because that was as close as Melanie would let her get to black.

Scratching his head, he called her cell. It was the first of many calls and voice messages to her phone that evening. Starting with, "Call me back please" and ending with "Where the hell are you?" After about the fifth call with no return, Jeff began to worry and tried remembering what was on her grocery list but he couldn't. He went to the pad in the kitchen, grabbed a pencil from out of the drawer and shaded the top page. He checked the cupboards; he checked the fridge. There wasn't any milk, eggs or cereal. She never came home from the store. He thought that maybe something had happened to the girls; maybe she had to leave the store and go straight to the neighbors.

He called up Kate, their longtime friend who hosted their sleepovers, the girls were fine and no she hadn't heard from Melanie since she dropped them off. He knew this wasn't like her, and he had no idea what to do next. His only option was to grab

Jack, put him in his Prius and drive over to the parking lot. There was a nip in the air; Jack had fallen back into a deep sleep on the car ride over. The security lights illuminated the lot to reveal only a few cars. Then he saw it, parked right beneath one of the lights dead center of the lot, Melanie's car. He drove around it and upon seeing no sign of her decided to pull over and go in for a closer look. He looked in the back window and saw all her bags sitting there but no sign of her. Out of the corner of his eye, a gold flicker. He looked down to see one gold sandal, and at that moment, Jeff knew she was gone.

He stared at it in disbelief, he knew what was next but dialing the numbers made it final. He ran his hand through his short blond hair, tugging at it a little to help relieve some of his anxiety. He tried Melanie's phone again in the hope that he was wrong. It went straight to voicemail. Her familiar voice filled his ears and told him that she was unavailable.

Even at this moment, her voice still turned him on; it was what drew him to her. It had that raspy tone that came from twenty years of smoking; only she was born with it. He didn't bother leaving a message. Instead, he called the Police and waited as instructed for them to arrive. He looked back at Jack, who was resting peacefully in his car seat. Jack looked more like his mother than him. He had her slightly curly brown hair and light skin. Jeff often wondered if his son would be tall like them. Melanie was very athletic and would not have had the best of her taken easily. She would have fought and fought hard. Jeff hoped that she didn't hurt herself trying to get away. He hoped she was still alive.

2

When Melanie finally came around with a pounding headache, she was cold and trussed up tighter than a Thanksgiving turkey. Her hands tied in front of her and her legs taped together. She was on something soft, she assumed a bed but couldn't see, something scratchy covered her eyes enough to obscure everything but not enough that she couldn't see a little or, at least, would have been able to if the room wasn't so dark. Melanie wanted to yell out but didn't, better she lay in wait quietly for what was to come. She thought about home and wondered if Jeff knew she was gone yet. Tears started to run down her cheeks when she thought about him and their girls, their son, Jack.

There was a creak off to her right; someone was coming. The door began to screech open; the sound was jarring. Melanie laid there as still as she could. She heard his footsteps coming across the floor.

Slide, scrape. Slide, scrape. Finally, he was beside her. The room was pitch black as she laid on her side facing away from the sound. She didn't dare turn over; she hoped he would believe she was asleep. He leaned over her; she could feel his hand gently parting her hair. The movement made every hair on her body stand on edge. There was a slight tug on the back of her hair followed by a cutting sound. Tears rolled down Melanie's face; she was so scared it was the only thing she could do. The bed which had once given way to his weight went back to normal. Again she heard the scraping noise that followed his feet across the room. The creaking door and then he was gone.

Melanie let out a sigh of relief as every muscle in her body started to relax again. She ached from head to toe but, at least, the migraine that she woke up with seemed to ease off. She tried to remember what had happened, but her mind was too fuzzy. Melanie figured he must have drugged her. She wondered what it was that he gave her, whatever it was it left her with one hell of a headache. She started to drift off to sleep again; her body was exhausted. She fought it off for as long as she could, desperate not to let down her guard.

****

"Melanie."

She could hear a voice calling to her, but she couldn't see who it was, it sounded like Jeff.

Melanie called out, "Jeff; I'm right here."

She walked around in the darkness looking for him until finally she came to a house that looked similar to hers. Melanie walked closer to the window and looked inside. She saw her girls and Jack much older than they are now, sitting around a table. The décor in the house was different, not her taste at all. She watched as Jeff wrapped his arms around another woman much younger than she. He kissed her on the back of the neck, and she giggled. The woman was holding a baby which Jeff took from her as he walked back to the table to join the girls.

Melanie banged on the window, but it made no sound. She yelled at the top of her lungs, but no sound came out, all she could hear was Jeff's voice but not the words he was saying to the pretty young woman in the kitchen that wasn't her. She screamed and banged some more, but it was for naught. They couldn't hear her; she didn't exist anymore.

Melanie woke up to the sound of screaming only to realize that it was her; she stopped when she remembered where she was. A voice filled the room; it sounded somewhat garbled as if it were coming through an intercom.

"Stop screaming."

There was a pause.

"I'm not going to harm you as long as you do what you're told."

With each pause Melanie waited for something to happen, she laid on the bed as still as she could muster, barely breathing from fear.

"You will be okay. I have no plans to harm you."

She wriggled around on the bed, assuming she could free herself but not wanting to make any noise while she did it. The bed started to creak, and she wondered if she was getting close to the edge. The last thing she needed was to fall off. The voice never returned, and she thought it was safe to assume he wasn't watching her. She could feel the rope around her wrists as she tried to wriggle them. It was no use; she would not be free until he freed her. She gave up on trying to free herself and instead decided to focus her energy on figuring out who took her.

She thought, if he were going to rape and kill me, he would have done it already. He wouldn't keep me locked up; he would have killed me already. Melanie tried her best to remember if she knew the voice but she couldn't place it, it wasn't familiar to her. She knew that to be the truth; she used to work with criminals all the time before becoming a stay at home parent. Melanie knew that it couldn't be any of them, they were lifers, sure to die in prison before release. She tried to think of someone, anyone who would want her taken, who would ransom her up. Unfortunately, two people came to mind.

3

It only took a few minutes for the swirl of flashing lights to surround Jeff in the Wal-Mart parking lot. He waved down the first arriving police officers who walked gingerly over to him and pronounced that the detectives on duty would be there shortly. They asked all sorts of preliminary questions, mostly getting a description that they could release to the media. Then the detectives showed up in their sedan and after giving the scene a once-over, they walked over to Jeff's Prius.

"I'm Detective Alvarez," said the portly and slightly balding man who was standing next to Detective Yates, who was also just as round and equally bald. Both were wearing almost the same exact suit, black with white shirts and blue ties. If it weren't for the racial difference, Jeff would have thought they were twins. "This is Detective Yates," he said gesturing to the man beside him.

"Babies can sleep through anything," Detective Yates remarked as he motioned to Jack in the backseat.

Detective Alvarez leaned up against the Prius, pulled out a pad and said, "Well, let's get started."

"Ok," Jeff mumbled.

Alvarez began with all the usual questions. A run-down of what happened until he arrived there.

"We're going to need an official statement made down at the station. Do you have anyone who can take the baby", Alvarez asked?

"Yes, my mother. I'll give her a call, but I need to go back to the house and get some things for him."

"Understandable. Here's what we will do. I need to get a team over to your house if that's okay with you?"

Jeff nodded, and Alvarez continued, "I'll send a few of my officers over to secure your house and sit there in case there's a call or she comes back. Yates will go with you and give you a ride to the station and start your statement."

Jeff nodded and followed the other officers and Yates to his home.

The house was still dark, but it felt more isolated and deserted than when he left it to find Melanie. It was almost depressing; it was as if he was walking into a stranger's house and not his home. He quickly packed some things for himself, Jack and the girls to take to his mother's house. He looked through pictures hanging around the living room, stopping in front of Melanie's law degree. Jeff had always wanted to be an attorney but after three disastrous LSATs, he gave up. It all came so easily to Melanie; she sailed through law school only to decide to become a social worker. Her Law degree taunted him every day on his way out of the door, everything Melanie wanted, she got, even him.

Jeff couldn't decide between the wedding picture where her hair was longer than it was now or a more current one that he knew she hated. Melanie wore her hair in a shoulder length bob now, and while he knew she would hate this picture plastered all over the news, he didn't have much choice. She looked very different with short hair. The officers that escorted him to the house stayed there, and once Jack was deposited at his mother's house, he made the slow drive across town to the police department.

Jeff waited for Yates in Detective Alvarez's office. The walls were covered with plaques and commendations, pictures with Alvarez and the Mayor. Jeff thought that with someone like Alvarez in charge they should find Melanie in no time.

Yates said as he came in and sat in his partner's chair, "Jeff, I won't take long. I just have a few questions, and I want to make sure I have everything I need to get started."

Jeff handed over the pictures he grabbed from the house while he was getting what he needed for Jack. "These are pretty recent."

Yates took them, went to the door and said something to a nearby Officer, who took the pictures. When Yates returned, sitting at the desk, he flipped through his notes before starting with his questions.

"We're going to get the picture out to the media to start circulating it. Is there anyone else, any of her family you'd like to contact before we get started?"

"No, she isn't exactly in touch with her family. Her immediate family is all dead."

"Okay. Fair enough. Around what time would you say Melanie left for the store?"

Jeff scratched his head; he wasn't sure, "Sometime between 6 and 8. It was still a little light out when she left."

"Between six and eight this evening, you were doing what?"

"I was watching TV and then I fell asleep on the couch." Jeff then added, "I was watching the Walking Dead.

The thought popped into his head that she was a pain in the butt too. He could never understand why someone would want to watch a show with you and then ask stupid questions about it the entire time? "I just wanted to watch my show, so I suggested she go to the store."

Jeff stared down at his hands, shaking his head. He wondered where she was at this moment, was she even alive? Feelings of relief and guilt washed over him and made him slightly nauseous. He needed something to drink. He excused himself briefly to get a cup of water from the cooler just outside the office. When he reentered, Yates was ready with another question.

"When we talked at the lot, you said you tried calling her but couldn't get through?"

"Yes. I called her multiple times, left messages, I even called Kate."

"Who is Kate?"

"Kate Murphy, she's a family friend, she had the girls tonight for a sleepover."

"What made you decide to go to the Wal-Mart?"

"It was the last place I knew she was going. I figured it was worth a try. If I wouldn't have found her car there, I guess I would have started calling hospitals or just would have called the Police because I have no idea where she would have gone."

"At this point, Jeff, we're going to do a few things. We're going to monitor her phone and credit cards to see if anything pops up. They didn't find a purse in her car or anywhere in the lot so we're going to assume for now she still has it. We're also going to see about getting that video from security and hope there's something on the tape that's useful. So what I suggest is, go to your Mother's and try to get some rest and if she calls or anyone else calls, let us know."

Jeff left the precinct, not believing that all this was happening and a little unprepared for what the next day would bring.

4

Another day had passed. She was wet, at some point during her drug-induced sleep she urinated on herself. Disgusted, she prayed that it would all be over soon. She heard the voice again and went still.

"Hello."

She said nothing.

"I would have figured you would have started to yell again once you woke up. I came in to check on you and make sure you were alright. Sometimes that stuff can give you a horrible headache. I have some pain reliever if you want it?"

"Oh how nice," she mumbled to herself but didn't dare say any louder. His voice was boyish, almost reluctant like an eleven-year-old when they try to 'man up' to their father. He was speaking very slow and calmly to her but instead of keeping her relaxed it just freaked her out more.

"Melanie, I want you to do something for me."

How does he know my name, she thought but answered a timid, "Yes."

"While you're here, your name is Brie, and that will be the only name you respond to, do you understand?"

She didn't respond.

"I've got plans for you Brie, very big plans," he said playing with her hair.

Melanie asked barely above a whisper, "What should I call you?"

"Brian."

She felt him lay a blanket on top of her, almost like he was tucking in a child. He ran his hands along her body from her shoulders down her legs to her feet. She tried not to shudder; she didn't want to do anything that might provoke him. She felt a slight pinprick, almost like an insect bite.

"Goodnight Brie, sleep well. I will make us breakfast in the morning."

Melanie heard the creak again, a chain, and then a lock bolting, and he was gone. She felt weak and was starving. The mere mention of food made her want to eat whatever was in sight. Her stomach growled in protest she needed, at least, some water. She wondered if he was going to starve her to death and what a horrible way to go that would be.

It became harder and harder for her to keep her eyes open, she figured he drugged her again. Melanie fought to keep her eyes open; she tried focusing on her kids. In her mind, she could hear Sara and Jenny fighting and Jack crying out for her. She wanted desperately to close her eyes and see them, but she was afraid to let go and let the drugs take over. Eventually, she would lose the fight and sleep would find her, stealing another day.

5

It was mid-day when Jeff finally got up the courage to pick up the girls. They would already know something was wrong by the fact that he was coming to get them and not Melanie. He told Kate to keep the TV off and the girls inside. On a beautiful day like today, that was not an easy task. It was fall, and there weren't that many days left of nice weather. He pulled up in front of the Craftsman style house that looked very similar to their own with its brick front, red door and the ever present wreath that was supposed to be welcoming.

"Hi Kate," Jeff said barely audible as he walked in the door and stood in their foyer. The smell of cooked bacon hit him immediately even though it had been a few hours since breakfast. Kate's home was always very tidy despite its shabby chic appearance; everything had a clearly labeled place.

"The girls are upstairs packing their stuff up. Have you figured out what you're going to say to them?"

"I wish I had nothing to say. They're fourteen, they aren't dumb, they have watched enough to TV to know how these things go, especially Jenny. No matter what I tell them, it's not going to reassure them that their mother is going to come home."

Jeff paused, hearing the floor creak upstairs and continued in a lower voice, "How can I reassure them when we both know she's probably lying in a hole somewhere?"

"Don't talk like that and definitely, don't let other people hear you talk like that."

Before Kate could finish, Jenny and Sara slowly walked down the steps like two people going on their last walk. Jenny the first down was closer to Jeff and more of a tomboy. Her very feminine appearance was always at odds with how she dressed. Even though they shared the same blond hair and blue eyes, Sara dressed the part and even side by side they looked like two different people who just happened to share the same face.

"Why are you here," Sara asked standing at the bottom of the stairs, at eye level with Jeff?

"Just go and get in the car okay. I need to talk to you guys. Thanks, Kate," He said as he ushered them out the door.

He knew he would have to tell them in the car before they got back to his mother's house and the circus that waited for them outside. Once they settled, he pulled off and drove to a nearby 7-11. The parking lot was packed, full of people stocking up on game day beer and ice for their football tailgating. He wound up having to park in the very back of the lot next to the dumpsters. The smell almost immediately entered the car through his rolled down window. He quickly made the adjustment and rolled up the window, turning on the A/C before facing the girls.

"What's going on, Dad," Jenny asked?

"Mom finally left him, Jenny," Sara said, "and obviously left us behind."

Stunned, Jeff asked, "Why would you even think that?"

"Because you spend more time out than you do at home, she thinks you're having an affair."

"How the hell would you know," Jenny spat back at her sister?

"I heard Kate talking on the phone with someone that she thought mom had left dad last night because he was having an affair."

"Enough," Jeff yelled, and they immediately stopped arguing. "Whether or not I'm having an affair is not the issue. Your mom is missing."

"So you are having an affair, what an asshole," Sara mumbled just loud enough for everyone to hear and sat back in her seat in a huff.

"I'm not having an affair and don't talk to me like that Sara. Your mom is missing. She never came back last night, and the cops found her car and not her. So we have to go to grandma's house for a little bit while the police search our house. There's going to be lots of cameras and people outside grandma's house when we get there so just try to ignore it."

"Why are the police searching our house? Did you kill mom?"

"Why would you even say that Sara," Jenny managed to stammer out through her tears. "Am I the only one who lives in this house,"

Sara yelled fuming as her eyes met Jeff's in the rearview mirror.

6

Melanie awoke, still groggy when she heard her faux name called. She had to remember to answer to it when called. It seemed important. Sometime during the night, when sleep finally found her, she was untied, her blindfold removed. Now, only a single thick chain connected her to the cuff locked around her ankle. The chain was long and went across the floor to a corner radiator. It had enough slack that she could walk around the room and use what Melanie assumed to be a little bathroom over in the corner. The room was gray, with one small square window situated high up on the wall and what little sunlight dared to venture through it, laid its warmth like a blanket across her face. There were only two doors. The he came through and the one to the bathroom.

"Good morning, Brie."

Melanie took a moment to size up her captor. He was just as tall as

Jeff, about 6'1 but very slim. He was a lot stronger than he looked. What struck her most is that he looked so normal. He would be the last person you would pick out of a lineup. His hair was a mix of blond and brown, his eyes the same color as hers. His appearance was almost comforting; it was as though she knew him from somewhere but just couldn't place him. It was his eyes, the shape of them and his chin that gave her a feeling of déjà vu that she just couldn't shake.

"I brought you some breakfast. I wasn't sure what you would like so I brought you a little bit of everything", Brian said as he set up a TV tray and sat her plate of eggs, pancakes, bacon and toast on the table.

She said, "I'm not hungry," because she was afraid to eat even though she was ravenous.

"Brie, breakfast is the most important meal of the day. You will eat and keep up your strength. I don't want you dying on me after I've gone to so much trouble to find you."

She looked down at the food and smelled it.

"I didn't poison it if that's what you're thinking," he said sitting next to her on the bed. "Come on and eat just a little." He picked up a forkful of scrambled eggs and held it to her mouth. She opened her mouth and slowly started to chew. Putting the fork in her hand, he proceeded to play in her hair while she ate.

"I'm so glad you're finally here Brie; I've been watching you for a long time. I had hoped you would notice me, but you never did. Then, there you were yesterday, all alone and I just couldn't help it. I had to bring you here, bring you home."

She continued to eat, slowly, just in case, there was something in it. Melanie waited for something to happen, but it didn't. He just kept talking and showing her all the things he had bought in preparation for her arrival, pretty dresses, and lingerie. He was giddy with a mirth only reserved for crazy people.

"When can I go home?"

"You are home."

"I need to go home, Brian. I have children that need me, a husband."

"Brie, I am all you'll ever need, we'll be a family soon enough."

"What do you mean, soon enough?"

"Don't worry about that now," he said changing the subject, "just eat."

"You have to let me go. I won't tell anyone. Just let me walk out", Melanie pleaded and reached out and grabbed his arm.

"You're not leaving," he yelled as he backhanded her across the face making her nose bleed. Startled, she knocked her plate and the remaining food onto the floor. She held her nose stunned, tears streaming down her face.

Calmer he said, "Brie, you are home. Now wash up, I'll clean up the mess and be back later."

He got up, cleaned the floor and took the tray making sure he had the fork. Then he shut and locked the door behind him. The weight of the chain was heavy as she dragged it across the cement floor. It made the most horrible scraping noise; she couldn't stand to hear it. For a little while, Melanie sat on the floor and cried. She thought about Jeff and how she missed him more now than she had ever missed anyone in her life. Her recollection of him was so strong that she could almost smell his musky vanilla scented cologne. She remembered how his arms felt around her the evening of their first date. Melanie could feel his embrace as he hugged her goodnight. A million little moments, his breath on her face, his lips on her neck. She missed him; she had to stay alive for him.

The bathroom was tiny only a shower stall, toilet, and sink. You could sit on the toilet and put your hand in the sink and your foot in the shower, a vast difference from the bathroom in her home. His and hers sinks, a Jacuzzi tub and a two person shower where Jeff and Melanie frequently made love. She smiled at the thought while she bathed. As the water ran down, she wondered if there was a way she could send a thought to Jeff to let him know she was okay, would he feel it. Would he know in his heart, she was still alive?

7

When Jeff and the girls arrived at his mother's house, it was a circus. News had already broken about the young wife, mother of three and daughter of the late oil magnate Harry Woodward, who went missing from a Wal-Mart parking lot. The video from the surveillance tape, already leaked to the press, showed a blurry man coming up from behind her and dragging her into his car. The video played every half hour in the hopes that someone would recognize the man or the car. The images were blurry; he looked like every guy you saw on the street. The angle wasn't good enough to get a license plate and was essentially useless.

Police had canvassed the neighborhood looking for anyone who might have seen or heard something. Hundreds of calls poured in, but there wasn't a single lead. Jack bounced in his jumpy seat oblivious to the chaos around him while Sara passed the time texting her friends on her iPhone. Jenny trailed behind Jeff following him where ever he went, afraid he would disappear too.

Sara asked Jeff, "How long are we going to have to stay here?"

"Until the police say we can go home. A few hours I hope but who knows, it could be days."

"What did you do to mom?"

"Why do you keep saying that? I didn't do anything to your mom", Jeff said putting his head in his hands, he was crying, but he didn't want Sara to see him doing it.

"Because we watch TV, the husband always does it."

He wiped his face and raised his head, "Just because you see it on TV then it must be true, right? How could you even think I would do that?"

"Her money, Dad. The will. All that money she got from Granddad when he died that she won't let you spend. All the money you argue over all the time. That's why you killed her."

Jeff just sat there, his mouth open; he didn't know what to say. He didn't even know that they had heard those arguments, all those fights about that stupid money. If anyone found out the truth, they would think he did it. They would think he killed his wife. But he didn't, Jeff knew he had to hold it together. He was an awful father and an even worse husband. If his kids thought he killed their mom, what would the police think?

"You shouldn't talk to you Father like that," Rose the girls' grandmother said. "Your Father couldn't harm a flea. He doesn't have it in him. Now you girls need to wash up and get ready for school."

Jenny was mortified, "You can't be serious. We can't go to school tomorrow."

"Oh, we're going," Sara said smiling. She would be Queen Bee tomorrow at school, and she wasn't going to miss it. She grabbed Jenny by the shirt sleeve and dragged her upstairs to get their things ready for school tomorrow.

Jeff sat in his mother's living room; it looked exactly as it had for the last 38 years. It was as much comforting as it was unnerving that anyone could stand seeing the same stuff for that long. He stared at his mother's upright piano that sat up against the living room wall. On top sat pictures of his children and their wedding picture. Finally, he broke down, not being able to hold it together any longer. The last person he wanted to see this was his mother but she was all he had left and he needed her.

"There, there Jeff. You need to pull yourself together," Rose said patting his shoulder before taking a seat beside him.

"The police are going to think I killed her. They're going to arrest me."

"You can't worry about that now dear. You just have to do what they tell you to do and in the meantime, I'm going to get you a lawyer."

"Won't that make me look guilty?"

"No, it won't. Not cooperating will make you look guilty. I'm not going to have my only child locked away for something stupid. Especially when there's no way you could have done it."

Jeff started to sob, and Rose wrapped her arms around him.

"But I am guilty, Mom. I often wished her dead."

"Hush now. Don't say things like that for people to hear."

Jenny sat at the top of the stairs and listened to it all before running to the bathroom to throw up.

8

The room had that sterile hospital smell only without the urine accompaniment. Melanie sat up in her bed and checked every inch of the room visually for a way out. She was too scared to get up and walk around, afraid the sound of her chain scraping the floor could be heard upstairs, and he would come back. As soon as that thought entered her head, she heard the locks unbolt and the loud creak as the door opened.

"Hello, Brie. How are you today?"

"My name is Melanie Tate."

Brian frowned and slammed the door hard behind him, the sound was so jarring it made Melanie jump.

"Your name is Brie. Are you hungry?"

"My name is Melanie Tate, and I have three children. I need to go home. Please, I promise I won't tell anyone a thing just let me go."

"You are here for me to keep you safe, Brie."

Frustrated, Melanie yelled, "I'm not Brie, I'm Melanie Tate."

The color of his eyes seemed to change and in that instant, Melanie knew she had pushed him too far. He traveled the expanse of the small room in two strides. He grabbed her by the throat and held her up against the wall choking her. She flailed, kicking her legs and waving her arms trying unsuccessfully to push him away. He was otherworldly strong; his appearance would deceive most people. Her chain scraped and clanged against the floor loudly as she went limp at the sound of his voice.

He said all too calmly, "I'm not a violent person, Brie. What is it going to take to get it through your mind that this is where you are staying?" He sat her down on the bed and watched as her hands immediately went to her throat and she gasped for breath. "There will be no food for Melanie Tate when Melanie decides she would like to be Brie; then we'll talk."

Before Melanie could look up he was gone, the door bolting behind him. She didn't know what to do, but that thought that he was going to kill her kept rolling around in her head. She was going to die and never see her family again. She pulled the blanket back over her head and laid down, crying until sleep finally found her again.

The room was pitch black when she heard the door opening again. She was starving and tossed most of the night from hunger pains. She heard his footsteps cross the floor and a tiny lamp click on beside the bed. It cast an eerie yellow hue across the room making it look like an insane asylum horror movie.

"Brie."

Melanie laid still and refused to move. She didn't want to give in if she was going to die she wanted to make it as difficult for him as possible.

He yelled, "Brie get up, now."

She rolled over and looked at his eyes which were barely visible in the bad lighting and said, "My name is Melanie Tate."

He then grabbed the blanket off Melanie and yanked her out of the bed by her arm; he dragged her to the wrought iron footboard of the bed. Grabbing her by the throat, he forced her to stand up. He let go of her throat just long enough to grab a pair of handcuffs out of his back pocket and lock her hands to the wrought iron footboard of the bed. It smelled old and musty.

"Bend over."

She did as he ordered and as she waited, she could hear him fumbling with his belt and then she felt it, the first whack to her back. The initial pain was horrible but the sting it left behind felt worse than the initial hit.

"Your name is Brie," he repeated each time before hitting her again with the belt.

By Melanie's count, he was up to fifteen before her legs began to shake and weaken from the pain. They finally gave out, and she hit her face on the metal bar of the bed, causing her nose and lips to bleed. She was sure her back was bleeding as well; her nightgown clung to her body. He continued to beat her even as she went down. She tried to curl up into a ball as best she could, but her arms were over her head and her one leg tethered to the chain.

Out of breath from the beating, he said one last time, "Your name.

Is Brie," Brian exhaled before collapsing on the floor next to her. Blood and snot mixed with the salt from her tears as Brian gently pushed her hair out of her face. He held her face in his hand and looked deep into her eyes. The yellow light is making them sparkle with an almost demonic ferocity, "Your name is Brie." Then he walked out, leaving her there, cuffed to the bed, bleeding.

9

Detective Yates and his officers spent the better of two days going over everything in the 3,500 square foot home. Yates, being the more senior detective was now in charge of what Burke Lake had deemed its high profile case. Alvarez was stuck working the murder across town that occurred the same night Melanie Woodward went missing. In the five days since her disappearance, there were no ransom demands. It led him to the belief that whatever happened to Melanie was not going to be good.

To Yates' dismay, the house was clean, but he expected as much. The bulk of their detective work accomplished via computers; he would now spend hours poring over phone records and analyzing whatever they found. He didn't believe Jeff did it, but he did believe that there was something that he was withholding. Melanie was worth more than 300 million dollars, and yet they lived in such a manner that befit the positions they held and not how much she was worth. Granted, she had only recently inherited the money. Her father passed away over five years ago, and yet the money sat there neatly allocated and barely touched.

The whole mess troubled Yates greatly; he hated not being able to solve a case and this one felt like it was going to be one of those cases that lingered on throughout the rest of his career, haunting him to find a resolution. He constantly made calls and checked messages, waiting impatiently for a ransom demand but five days went by and he was itching for a break.

Yates flipped open his cell and called his assistant Judy, "it's time to talk to the vultures," His message was brief, but Judy knew it meant to call for a press conference. All he had to do was convince Jeff to go on the TV to talk about his wife and just maybe whoever had her might pop their head up. Yates flipped open his phone yet again to call Jeff, who was still asleep on his mother's couch.

Rose nudged Jeff awake, "Your phone is ringing".

Jeff rolled over and picked it up, "Jeff."

"Jeff, this is Detective Yates. I need you to come to the station at one this afternoon."

"For?"

"We're having a press conference, and we need you there."

"I don't feel comfortable talking to the press," Jeff started before Yates interrupted him.

"It's not an option; I'll need you down here at one. I would think you'd want to do anything you could to find your wife."

Jeff had started to say, "Yes", but Yates had already hung up the phone.

Jenny walked over to her dad and gave him a hug as Sara stood in the entryway and watched, typing something into her cell phone.

"See you later Dad, Grandma Rose is giving us a ride to school; we're already late."

"Goodbye girls," Jeff said as he watched Sara roll her eyes before walking out behind Jenny.

Jeff stood next to Detective Yates in a small room that was set up for the press conference. They were crammed into a room no bigger than a very large executive office that contained a podium and about fifty white folding chairs. As soon as he walked into the room flashes started going off until the crowd settled and Detective Yates began to speak.

"I just want to make a brief statement, and then Mr. Tate has something he would like to say, we'll have a very brief Q&A after that."

Jeff shifted his weight from one side to the other trying his best not to do anything that would make him look guilty. He didn't smile and was too nervous to cry.

Detective Yates started, "Melanie Woodward Tate has been missing for approximately five days going by the time stamp on the video. The Burke Lake Police Department would like to send a message directly to the person or persons that are holding Mrs. Tate. The family is willing to negotiate. As of right now, neither the family nor the Police Department has received any demands. We require proof of life sent along with any demand for payment for her safe return. The family is also issuing a reward of $50,000 to anyone who has information that would lead directly to the safe return of Mrs. Tate and/or the apprehension of the person or persons responsible. Thank you."

Cameras began to flash as Jeff took to the podium; he stood there for a minute, not knowing what to say really. He knew what he should say but all he could think about at the precise moment was the fact that Detective Yates just offered $50,000 of his family's money without discussing it all with him.

"I just wanted to take this opportunity to thank everyone who has come out to help my family and me. You've been awesome, and we are just so very grateful. I want to tell my wife if she's watching this, we're looking for you and to whoever took you, contact me so we can reunite Melanie with her kids."

Jeff stepped back from the podium, and Yates walked back to his place to begin fielding questions from the journalists. Sally Martin, from the local news, sat in the audience listening to all the other reporters ask the same questions that she knew in advance they wouldn't get answers to. Right before she was about to raise her hand to ask a question her phone dinged and an image flashed across her screen. It was a screenshot from her producer of a tweet sent by Jeff's daughter, Sara, right after Melanie disappeared. It read, "If the cops search the back yard my dad is screwed. #orangeisthenewblack."

Sally couldn't believe what she was reading. She had to use this; it was a total scoop. She didn't want to be that type of journalist, but she also needed a raise. Being on the frontline of a story when it broke was going to up her status at the network.

Sally raised her hand, and when Detective Yates called on her, she stood up, and after she had introduced herself she asked, "Detective Yates, have the police concluded the search of the house?"

"Yes, we have."

"I recently came into the possession of a tweet from Jeff's daughter that says, if they look in the backyard Dad is screwed. Have the police searched the backyard?"

Floored, Jeff stood there looking at Yates, who glared at him but only said, "No comment, the session is over."

"What would the police find if they looked in the backyard, Jeff? Would they find Melanie there", Sally yelled as she watched

Detective Yates grab Jeff by the arm and usher him out of the room, cameras flashing the entire time.

"What the hell was that? How is that supposed to help me find my wife? That tweet was from a fourteen-year-old girl that hates me," Jeff yelled at Detective Yates out in the hallway, "you can't seriously think my wife is in my backyard."

"Jeff, we need to talk to the girls. You can't expect me not to take this seriously even if it is from a fourteen-year-old that hates you. We can't talk to them without your permission, but it would go a long way towards cooperation if you'd just let us talk to them. You can have your lawyer present if you'd like."

"Whatever. I'll bring them by tomorrow."

Yates paused as if he was pondering something important and then said, "I'd like to do that now if you don't mind, I'll send a car over to the school to pick them up and bring them here. You can sit in the interrogation room until they get here."

"Should I call my lawyer?"

"That's up to you," Yates said quickly before leaving Jeff in the interrogation room.

10

She yelled for him to come, for hours with no response.

Eventually, she gave in to her basic needs and urinated on the floor

because she could no longer hold it. She yelled at him again but no

answer. Eventually, her throat sore, she fell asleep. Light began to

stream in from the tiny window above her, boring into her eyelid

and forcing her awake. Still locked to the bed in a puddle mixed

with urine and blood turning the edging of her nightgown a light

orange, she squeezed her eyelids together in an attempt to force out

the stinging left behind when one runs out of tears. Her face was

sore, but she couldn't quite tell if there was swelling, it felt like it

was. She tried to cry out for him, to relent but all that came out was

a weakened croak. The bolts started their familiar unlocking

sequence as Melanie became rigid.

"Brie."

Brie raised her head and looked at him. In his hands, he had a towel folded neatly and on top of a rather large first aid kit. Brian

went into the bathroom and filled a small basin he kept under the

sink with warm water. After unlocking the cuffs, he began to clean

her up very slowly and as gentle as he could. Once he washed her

face and inspected it for any cuts, he helped her up off the floor

and into the bathroom. He pulled the wet nightgown off as gently

as he could and turning on the shower, left her in the bathroom to

wash up.

While she showered, Brian cleaned the floor, the smell of

antibacterial floor cleaner filled the small room again. She emerged

from the shower in the white bathrobe he placed in there, her back

still stinging from the night before. He motioned for her to come

over to the bed, where he handed her some clothes and turned

away so she could dress.

Brie sat there on the edge of the bed dressed in a very simple

flowered dress and a pale pink sweater that she pulled over the top.

She pulled her shoulder length brown hair back with a hair clip.

The clothes he picked to fill her closet were very feminine and

lacy, almost delicate. Not her usual attire at all, but she liked it. It was how she wished Jeff would see her sometimes, lacy and full of femininity instead of the task master she had become.

"Brie."

"Yes."

Kissing her forehead, he said, "Very good, love. I'll be back in a bit."

It had seemed like half of the day had slipped by before he came into her room again with a bottle of wine, two glasses and a plate of cheese and crackers. On his tray, a single bud vase with a solitary white rose still closed. He sat the tray in front of her and sat beside Brie as he had before, taking the flower out of the vase and handing it to her. Today, a little more disheveled, his brownish blond hair not slicked back as it was the day before. It hung loosely on his face, and he tucked it back behind his ears before pouring the wine.

"I cut this from our garden, especially for you, a peace offering. There was a time when the color of the flower and the number of them was significant. A single rose meant that the giver was devoted to the recipient and white meant that the person giving the rose was worthy of the love of the recipient. In my own small way, I'm apologizing, and I hope that you will forgive me."

She sat there motionless and unresponsive but took the flower, smelled it and then placed it back into the vase.

"Is your face ok," he asked as he tried to reach out to touch Brie's face but she instinctively leaned away.

"It's fine."

"Please join me. If you're hungrier, I can make you something else. I didn't know if you would be hungry or not."

Brie started to eat. She wished she was comfortable enough to drop her guard and have some wine. She just wanted to be numb, to have the all-over tingly feeling that comes after you finish a glass of Merlot. He saw her staring at the bottle and motioned for her to have some. Brie shook her head.

"No worries, I'm not about to get you drunk and take advantage of you. Now is not the time for that," Brian said as he gave her a glass.

The wine, though not the best she had ever tasted was good enough to do the job. It made her relax while she listened to him ramble on about medieval traditions. His voice was so soft and gentle it matched his minuscule frame. When he was angry, he became another person entirely. His light hair seemed to turn black, and his frame enlarged to match his emotions. When he was calm, he looked as docile and as insignificant as a church mouse. He wasn't horrible to look at either. A normal guy, there was nothing about him to make him stand out from the man next to you in the checkout line. Melanie knew that Brie was going to have to play his game. She was going to have to "love" him to be free again. Could she find something worthy of love in a man who was so undeserving?

Brie asked because the wine gave her courage, "Why me"?

"One night, a long time ago, I had a dream, and it was you. My life was perfect again, and I just had to live in that dream with you. Then one day, like magic, there you were. I followed you home, and I watched you. I saw you standing at the sink in your kitchen crying after getting off the phone. I knew then that you were unhappy too. I knew if we could be together we would both be happy; it would be like my dream."

Brian poured her another glass and played in her hair; Brie started to cry. He moved closer to her, but she leaned away, a little afraid of what he was going to do. He cupped her face in his hands and saying nothing; he wiped away her tears with his thumbs, pulled her close to him and gave her a long hug. She laid against his chest limp with her arms at her sides, waiting for his release. His scent was comforting, a mix of sweet and musky. His embrace was warm and inviting.

"You can hug me back if you want," he said.

She wasn't exactly sure if it was an invitation or order, so she did, her back still stinging with each exaggerated movement.

"I will never hurt you again. I love you, but you can never leave," he said as he released her and stared into her eyes.

"You can't keep me locked in this room forever."

"That's exactly what I plan on doing."

"Why?"

He got up and started cleaning but never answered her question. When he had gathered everything and did his routine check to make sure he was leaving nothing behind that Brie could use while he was gone. He turned to leave.

"Why," she asked again as he walked toward the door?

"Because I can," he whispered then shut the door behind him.

11

Brie tossed in her bed before jumping awake. She thought she could hear Jack crying; she was sure of it. The connection between her and her children was so strong that she knew what they sometimes needed before they were even aware. She had gone through so much to have them. The years of infertility had taken its toll on her and her marriage. Before she received her inheritance, all they had was their savings. The IVF treatments were the only time she gave in and used their considerable savings on something. After quite a few rounds of IVF, she had her daughters and then again with Jack. The thought of what they must be feeling overwhelmed her and made her determined to survive.

Brie sat on the floor next to bed crying silently because she didn't want him to hear. She wanted out of there; she just couldn't see a way out. Would he ever let her go? Would she have to comply with his wishes first?

Brie heard the lock and bolt click. He was returning. This time, he had a box, wrapped in shiny pink paper adorned with a ribbon.

"Brie, I bought this for you," He said handing her the box.

She took the box and slowly opened it. Inside was a pale pink silk nightgown with very delicate lace around the neckline and a matching robe, all in her size.

"Tomorrow, I have to go to work. I'll leave you with some food in the morning. Mostly snacks and things you can eat without utensils. I have some books and magazines you might also like to read to pass the time. I installed a bell that is located outside your bedroom door, and when I get home, I will ring it to let you know that I am back. When you hear the bell, I want you to put this on and wait for me to come down to have dinner with you."

Brie mumbled, "Okay," as if she were a child taking orders. She placed the clothes back in the box and sat them on the bed. He left but came back quickly with the books another tray of food with plates for the both of them.

"We have a few more things to go over," he said as if he were reading a speech he had prepared, "First, the door is rigged. If you tamper with it at all, even jiggle the handle an alarm will sound on my phone. The same thing goes for the window as well."

He pulled out his Samsung phone and showed her.

"I created my own app. It tells me everything that goes on in this room while I'm away. If you flush the toilet, I'll know about it. So for your sake, be good."

Brie ate in silence listening to rules as he described them. When he finished, he watched her eat and slowly stroked her hair. It was odd the way it didn't bother her as much as it had two days before. Now accustomed to his touch, he noticed that she didn't flinch as she normally did and drew closer to her. His hand stroked her cheek, Brie put down her sandwich and sat there waiting to see what he would do next. Brian felt her go rigid and dropped his hand back to his plate and continued to eat. When they finished, he collected everything and sat it on the tray, placing it by the door. He returned to the bed and standing over her asked Brie to go shower and prepare for bed.

Obligingly, she got up, grabbed a cotton nightgown from the makeshift dresser and went into the bathroom. The water was warm and relaxing, for a brief moment she could pretend she was at home. Brian's tapping on the door startled her, and she knew it was time to get out. Brie quickly dried and dressed, not wanting to keep him waiting. She walked past him, over to the bed and after getting under the blanket, Brian laid down beside her. She could feel his breath on the back of her neck.

He whispered, "I will miss you tomorrow while I'm away. For your sake, please don't do anything stupid. You're mine now, and I love you, Brie."

Before getting up to leave, he pushed her hair away from her face and kissed the back of her neck. The bed shifted when he got up, but she didn't turn to see him leave. The door bolted shut again.

The next morning he did as he said he would. Brian left her breakfast and some snacks to pass the day. He left Brie, a bunch of girlie magazines he thought would interest her because he didn't know any better. The books he left were all romance novels from the local library, about women held captive and falling in love with their captors. Each cover looked the same, a beautiful woman with an equally attractive man, the wind blowing through their hair. It was then; as she looked at the cover, Brie had an idea, a way out. Eventually, he would take these books back to the library and check out more. All she had to do was slip a note inside, hidden well. Maybe someone else would check it out, find the note and call the police. It was a long shot, but it was the only chance she had at the moment. The day got a little brighter as she laid on the bed and started to read.

12

In his office building, Brian stood in the entry way to the break room watching the press conference on TV. He kept his phone in his pocket on vibrate and periodically checked the app to see what she was doing. At that moment, the video feed from her room showed her reading one of the library books. He smiled to himself as his assistant pulled him aside to remind him of a meeting.

"It really is sad about that woman," Maxine, Brian's assistant said in passing.

"They'll find her. Eventually, someone will stumble across her in the woods would be my guess," Brian said nonchalantly, "Husband probably murdered her for the money."

Maxine playfully hit Brian in the arm for saying such a thing, but she knew it was true. He hated when Maxine touched him. It was annoying, but he endured it. He even playfully joked with her once, that her constant need to grope people was sexual harassment, she never got the hint, so he left it alone. It wasn't normal to not want to be touched and above all else, he had to be normal. Brian held the conference room door open for her as he checked his phone one last time before directing the meeting.

Being locked away gave her too much time to think, for a while everything was just a blur of muddy scenes in her head. What did she do wrong, why didn't she see him coming? These thoughts tormented her all day. She read the books and thumbed through magazines to keep the thoughts at bay. There was no use in replaying it in her mind. She couldn't change her situation, and she was afraid to test the limits of her confinement.

She remembered walking through the store. Did he follow her then, she didn't know. Was he even with her in the store? Was he waiting outside of it for her to come out? She couldn't recall seeing a car behind her on the way to Wal-Mart. He was there, waiting for her to drop her guard just enough to take her away. She walked out to her SUV and began loading the bags. She remembered hearing footsteps but she was in a parking lot and ignored them, she thumbed through her purse for the car keys and to make sure she didn't leave her credit card in the store.

It was then that two arms quickly embraced her, one over her face covering her mouth, the other around her waist dragging her backward. Tightly bound by him she kicked to no avail. She couldn't remember going into the trunk; she was out cold by then, just a lump of flesh still clutching her purse and keys. The car gingerly drove away, revealing nothing of the commotion that just occurred.

She quickly jumped up off the bed, the chain scraping the floor behind her, and looked around for her purse and keys. She checked the drawers, nothing. Looking under the bed she saw one of her sandals, its mate, lost. Then, she remembered it flew off while she was kicking her feet. At least, she left a clue behind, she thought, she was almost like Cinderella except this was no fairytale, and he was no prince. She sat back on the bed, resigned to the fact that she would have to wait it out. Time was the only thing she wasn't quite sure she had.

13

It wasn't long before Jenny was walking into the interrogation room as her father sat in an adjacent office and waited.

"Hi Jenny, I'm Detective Yates," he said extending his hand to her and shaking it. "I've brought you here to ask you some questions about your parents. Your father is right outside of this room and at any time if you don't feel comfortable, or you want to stop we can go and get him, okay?"

Jenny nodded and then said, "Yes" when Yates pointed to the microphone.

"Jenny, let's just get right down to it. Do you think your father harmed your mom?"

"No."

"Why do you say that?"

"Because he loves her."

"Did your parents fight a lot?"

"They would go a while and not fight at all then something would happen, and they'd really fight a lot for like, a week, and then everything would go back to normal."

"Do you love your dad?

"Of course, I do," Jenny said her voice pitched slightly higher, she considered the question absurd.

"Jenny, I asked you that question because sometimes people we love do things that we know are wrong but we love them so much that we just want to help them."

"You mean, you think I would lie so he wouldn't get in trouble?"

"Yes, that's exactly what I mean, so would you?"

Jenny paused, she thought about the other night when she sat on the steps and heard her father talk about how he wished their mother dead. She knew if she told Detective Yates that he would have even more reason to think that he did something to her mom. He wouldn't understand, and she couldn't tell him.

Yates noticed her reluctance to answer and changed the subject to her sister, Sara. "Jenny, Sara posted a tweet after your mom went missing that said the police should dig up the back yard. Do you know why she posted something like that?

Jenny quickly said, "She likes the attention and she doesn't care that it will hurt Dad. There's NOTHING in our backyard except flowers and dirt and Sara knows that."

"Thank you, Jenny," Yates said excusing her from the room. "Tell your sister she can come in now."

Sara walked in like she owned the place, texting rapidly as she walked. Detective Yates gave her the same introduction that he had given Jenny twenty minutes prior. She took her seat and gave out a little sigh as she did so.

"Why did you send the tweet?"

"Because you guys barely went through our house, my mother is missing, she's loaded, and there's been no one asking for money. Doesn't that seem strange to you?"

"Yes, it does. It seems very strange. But you didn't answer the question as to why you sent the tweet? Yates asked trying to prod her along, "Did you see something?"

"No, I didn't see anything. I was at a friend's house which is pretty convenient don't you think?"

"Convenient, how?"

"Ms. Kate's daughter, Iris, is my friend. Usually, when we have a sleepover, Jenny never comes, she stays home with dad. Now all of the sudden, I have to bring her along, which is fine, whatever. I just thought they wanted to have their 'alone time.' So we went over to stay with Iris, and he's home with mom and Jack and Jack's a baby so what does he know."

"I would say that sounds convenient," Yates said taking notes like a fiend of all the questions he wanted to follow up with before he forgot but he started with, "Were your parents fighting before you left or maybe even the day or week before?"

"I don't remember them having a fight that day, but I do remember them fighting, but they would always stop if they thought we could hear."

"Do you remember any specifics fights?"

"At one point, mom thought dad was cheating on her so they would fight about that but mostly they just argued about her money. He wanted her to use it for something, and she wanted to save it for us."

"Do you think your dad did something to your mom, is that why you sent the tweet?"

"I don't think my dad could harm anyone at least not by himself," Sara said as she stood, "Can we be done now cause I really gotta pee."

Yates pointed in the direction of the restroom and said, "Yes, we're done for now."

Detective Yates sat at the table and looked over his notes. Under Jenny he wrote, closer to the father knows something more but will never tell. Under Sara he wrote, check bank records again, look for information that father might have hired someone, check the house again.

While the girls sat together in a nearby office, Jeff went into the interrogation room.

Yates began, "I'd like to formally question you about a few things if that's alright with you Jeff?"

"It's fine."

"Ok, let's get started. First things first, we need your permission to search your house again and your Prius and a few other things, is that ok?" Jeff nodded but again did not speak.

"The day of Melanie's disappearance, walk me through it."

Jeff sat back in his chair and tried to remember everything; he tried to picture her in his mind. He hadn't paid much attention to how she looked that morning when she went out on her run. He couldn't even tell the officers what she was wearing when she left the house that day because he never even looked at her. He just gave her a sideways kiss before returning to his show.

"We got up, went through our routine. I made breakfast for the kids, and she went out for a run."

"Does Melanie have a regular route or trail that she runs?"

"I have no idea. I would assume she runs the trail because it goes right to our house but I don't know."

"Does she run alone?"

"Again, I don't know. I think she does."

"What happened the rest of the day?"

"I did chores around the house, like cutting the grass and stuff and she took the girls over to Kate Murphy's to spend the day and sleep over. I put Jack to bed, and we had an early dinner. We started to watch TV. She was bored, so I suggested she run her errands."

Yates wrote a note to himself to check Jeff's phone records for the time Melanie was at Kate Murphy's and while she was at the store. Then asked, "What time did she leave?"

"Like I said before, it was sometime around 6; I don't remember exactly when."

"After your wife left, you stayed at home watching TV?"

"Yes, then I must have fallen asleep."

"Sometime after six, you fell asleep and didn't wake up again until after 11?"

"Yeah, something like that."

Jeff watched Yates make another note. He desperately wanted to know what the hell he was writing down. It made him nervous, all this note taking like he was saying something wrong. The whole situation was making him nervous. He thought back to that night; he knew he went out for about a half an hour after Melanie left. He was in and out; he made sure not to linger too long because he wanted to be back home by the time Melanie got back. He knew he had about an hour. The thought of that night almost pushed a smile to come to his lips, he resisted the urge and asked the Detective to repeat his question.

"Was there anything different about that day, anything at all you can remember?"

"No, it's like I said. The girls were at a sleepover and Melanie, and I was going through our normal routine. Then I suggested she go to the store since Jack was asleep, she could get it out of the way."

"So that wasn't her normal routine?"

"No, it wasn't. She usually went on Sunday morning; she hated driving at night."

"You said the reason you suggested she deviate from her routine was because the baby was sleeping?"

"Yeah, Jack went to sleep early, and I was watching TV. She doesn't like to watch TV and seemed bored, so I suggested she get out the house and get the shopping done. That way I could watch my show in peace."

"So she leaves and then what happened and was there anyone who saw her leave besides you?"

"I don't know if anyone else saw her leave. All I remember was she came over to me, said she was leaving and grabbed her keys and left. I was watching TV, so I didn't see her pull out the driveway, but I heard the car leave. After that, I watched TV until I fell asleep. I woke up, and the house was dark. I called Kate, who was keeping the girls after I tried Melanie a few times and got no response. After that I figured out she never came back from the Wal-Mart, so I went there, found the car and called the cops."

"How did you know she never came back from the store?"

"I checked the fridge and the pantry. I didn't see anything new in there, so I thought it was safe to assume she never came back from the store."

"Did you argue that day?"

"No, not that I can remember."

"Do you argue at all?"

"We've had our fights, nothing horrible, just marital disagreements. The police have never been called to the house if that's what you mean."

"Does Melanie have any enemies or someone she just doesn't get along with, maybe even as far back as her old job?"

"I don't think so, and if she did, she didn't tell me. Melanie was…I mean is well liked, even when she worked for the Department of Corrections everyone liked her."

"In her role as a social worker for the prison, do you think there was anyone who liked her too much? Maybe an inmate she worked with?"

"What's that supposed to mean?"

"You know what I mean, Mr. Tate."

Jeff becoming increasingly more annoyed said, "If you think my wife was having an affair and ran off, she wasn't. You saw her shoe in the parking lot same as me. Her car was unlocked, and all her stuff was in it. Instead of insinuating something underhanded was going on, which I know is what usually happens in these situations, you need to treat it as an abduction, cause that's what it is. My wife might want to leave me, but she would not leave her kids."

"Look, Jeff, I'm just trying to get to the bottom of what happened to your wife, to find her. Every piece of information you give me could be something that could help me locate her. I'm sorry if you find my questions annoying, but I'm just trying to do my job."

"I'm sorry, I'm just tired."

"Why don't you take your girls and go on home. If I have some follow-up questions, I'll pop over to your house."

Jeff got up and was escorted down the hall to where the girls were. They sat opposite one another the entire time, Sara on her phone and Jenny drawing an intricate tattoo on her hand.

The car ride home was silent. The girls went back to their old rooms and tried to settle in even though the house just didn't feel the same. Jack was remaining with Rose for the time being until she could close up her house and come to stay with them. Jeff dropped their bags and walked directly into his study. He glanced around at all the items strewn about; they rummaged through everything in his office. He was almost positive they'd found it, but he had to know for sure. He pulled the bottom drawer all the way out of his desk and felt along the back wall; it was still there! He couldn't believe his good luck, he ripped the tape off the phone and turned it on. All he could think about was, he had to delete the messages and all the pictures. Then he would get rid of the phone. It wasn't enough to just throw it in a lake or a dumpster; he had to be sure that he erased everything. One by one he deleted every single message from him to Mike Neil.

14

The day dragged slowly for Brian; he wanted to be home with Brie. As he watched the clock on his office wall tick for the last four hours of his work day, he fielded calls, ran meetings and acted like his normal affable self. His colleagues would never have thought that when he whipped out his phone in meetings that he wasn't checking his email but the movements of the woman he was keeping chained up in the basement.

At five o'clock Brian jumped up from his desk, bag already packed and walked quickly down the cubicle lined hallway, hoping that he would be able to make it to the elevators without someone stopping him to ask one last question. The elevator doors closed behind him as he made his way through the garage and over to his black Infiniti. Before he pulled out of the parking garage, he checked his phone one last time and then started for home.

He stood in front of the mirror in his entry way just staring at himself. He took his suit jacket off, studied himself only to put it back on again and then eventually taking it off, hanging it over the back of his old green side chair. He wished he could just bring her upstairs. He wanted to walk in the door after work and see her there waiting for him instead of down in his basement, chained like an animal. He didn't want to do that, but he knew he had to; there was no other way to keep her safe. He was saving her and sometimes, the end justified the means.

Brian rang the bell and Brie jumped out of her skin; she had not expected the time to fly so fast. She expected to spend the day bored to tears but knowing he was gone made it easy for her to relax. She relaxed so much so that eventually it was evening and it was time for the farce to begin. The ring of the bell startled her; she didn't know how much time she had to get ready, so she quickly jumped out of bed. She was dressed for dinner by the time she heard the familiar unlatching of the door.

Brian carried in Chinese takeout; it smelled heavenly to her, and Brie could not wait to start eating. Brian could tell by the look on her face that she liked Chinese food, and she was probably starving. Her happiness with something so simple made him smile. For a moment, he thought, this might actually happen this time.

"Today was a wonderful day, Brie," he said as he stroked her hair, pulling it back into a ponytail and then letting it fall again. She had become accustomed to him playing in her hair and even though she thought his obsession with it odd, it didn't bother her as much anymore. If playing in her hair kept her alive, she would welcome the touch and hope he didn't want more.

Brian wished she would just engage; he was so impatient, all the psychology books he read told him that it took months for someone to have positive feelings towards their captor. It was a process that he couldn't rush, but he longed to be able to unchain her and come home to the family he wanted so desperately.

"Do you like your dinner?"

"It's very good," Brie said trying to not to be disgusting, her mouth full of fried rice. "Where did you get it?"

Brian quickly blurted out, "It's that little place around the corner from your house," before he realized what he was saying.

"You've been back to my neighborhood? Why?"

Trying to deflect, he said, "I haven't, I just went to get the food because I thought you might like it."

"You have been back there. What's going on? Are my kids okay? Have you seen them?"

"I haven't seen anything."

"You have! Please just tell me. I know you're watching the news, are they even looking for me, have you seen the kids on TV, have you seen my husband?"

Brian thought for a few moments on how best to answer her questions. She was right; he had watched the press conference on TV. He followed the case as it developed, wanted to know everything that he could about it. On his way to work, he would pass by her house just out of curiosity.

"I only saw the kids, briefly. They are staying with his family. That low life you call a husband wasn't even upset on the TV, he just stood there looking like the jerk that he is."

"He loves me, and he's looking for me."

"The only thing he cares about is how soon he can have access to your money."

"You can have my money, all of it. I never wanted it anyway. Just release me. I'll say, I didn't know who you were or where I was. I'll give them no information, and I'll just transfer the money to you, and you can go live on an island somewhere."

"This isn't about the money."

Brie completely exasperated asked, "Then what is it about?"

"It's about you, us, family. That's what this is about", Brian said taking Brie's hand and holding it up to his mouth to kiss it. "I want to take care of you, keep you safe and be your family."

Brie continued to eat in silence, the spot where he kissed her hand still felt warm. Melanie would have pulled her hand away from him before he had the chance to kiss it but to Brie, his touch was comforting. It reminded her of when she would breastfeed Jack when he was an infant. He would snuggle with her, and the rise and fall of his chest would just relax her. He had the ability to put you at ease with only his presence. Her daydream cut short as she watched Brian, deep in thought, pacing back and forth, muttering to himself, he was starting to look crazy. She never realized he had left her side. It hadn't occurred to her what she did to set him off, but she had wished she hadn't. She was scared to speak; not knowing what would set him off or calm him down.

Finally, she dared to say, "Would you like to play a game with me? There's Scrabble or Checkers over there in the corner. It might be fun to pass the time." She had discovered the games beside the dresser when she was looking for her purse. She dared not ask him what he did with it.

Brian stopped pacing; this was the thing he was most waiting for, a little interaction. He grabbed the Scrabble game and sat down, cross-legged in front of her on the bed. He set up the game, gave her the bag of tiles and began playing.

"You know, I'm really good at this game, so don't get mad if you lose," Brie said trying to sound like she was having a good time.

Brian, playing along stated, "The only way you'll win, is if I let you."

"Okay, we'll see."

As they sat there playing the game and challenging each other over every obscure word, Brian wished that it could have always been like this. Why couldn't it have been him, he wondered? Every failed relationship he had ever had, he often wondered what the missing piece was. Then suddenly, there she was. His purpose in life was now her, and he was determined he would not fail. Brian would keep her safe; he would have his family, no matter what the cost.

"I've got to work in the morning, I wish we could do this all night but I've got to get to bed," Brian said rubbing his eyes. He began cleaning up from dinner and the game while Brie went into the bathroom. The door to the bathroom was slightly ajar, and he could see her reflection in the mirror. To him, she was the most beautiful woman in the world, and he longed just to be able to walk in behind her and put his arm around her waist. He imagined himself doing so, Brie walked out and jolted him back to reality as the chain around her ankle dragged loudly across the floor.

"I wish I didn't have to have that horrible thing around your ankle," Brian said walking over to her bed, to say goodnight.

"Then take it off of me."

"It's for your own good. I have to keep you here, keep you safe," he leaned over her and brushed her hair away from her face, kissing her forehead. He flicked the light switch next to her bed and for a moment the room was completely dark, the soft glow of the moonlight coming through the tiny window began to make the shapes in the room visible again.

"Goodnight, Brian."

He paused briefly to look at her lying there, taking a picture with his mind to recall later when he would lay in his bed alone. He wanted so badly to kiss her goodnight but was afraid. The fear of her turning away or worse slapping him kept him from doing what he wanted to do. He simply said, "Goodnight, love" and left the room, turning the locks behind him.

15

Detective Stan Yates hated every aspect of being an officer, so he did the climb to Detective in record time only to discover he hated that as well. Seeing the worst of humanity day in and day out had done things to him over his fifteen years on the force. He counted his waistline as the collateral damage that the war of protecting and serving had taken from him over the years. He hated the rain and today it was pouring buckets. In fact, Stan Yates could name more things he hated than he enjoyed, his current case would be high up on that list.

In the week that passed since Melanie Tate's abduction, he had given more press conferences than he cared to. He didn't want this case; he liked to work behind the scenes. He was in the wrong place, at the wrong time Yates his whole life and this case was no exception.

When he stepped out of the patrol car and into the storm, he half walked, half jogged up the steps of Kate Murphy's house. She was on his list of people to interview, and the fact that he was just making his way around to her would have been appalling to the other detectives but he worked cases like this slowly, and he wasn't accustomed to working alone.

Kate was expecting Yates' arrival, ushering him in to get out of the storm. She gave him a quick tour of the downstairs portion of the house before asking him if he wanted anything. When he declined, they settled in her office. Or at least, that's what she called it; it looked more like a mini library that contained a desk. Books were strewn everywhere and upon closer inspection looked as though they were never touched once they reached their final destination. The office, never used for actual work, was more of a place where books went to languish until they were sold for fifty cents at her next garage sale. Kate was a master illusionist, and this room gave the impression that she was an avid reader when nothing could be further from the truth.

"Ms. Murphy, How long have you known the Tate's?"

"They moved to this neighborhood when my husband and I were still married a few years before they had their girls, so close to 15 years I think."

"Where you close to Melanie?"

"We were friends; I would say we've gotten closer in the last 6 or so years. Initially, when we met, I was having marriage difficulties, so I wasn't that close to anyone. She helped me a lot after the divorce. She helped me keep my house."

Yates, interrupted, "She helped you keep your house?"

"Yes, after my divorce. She helped me with a few of the mortgage payments," Kate said crying. "I hope you find whoever took her and nail his ass to the wall because she was a nice person."

"Was?"

"Is, she is a nice person. I'm just so afraid; it's been so long. Do you think she's dead?"

"I'll be honest with you; it doesn't look good."

Kate took a tissue from the holder on her desk and blotted her eyes. Yates looked away to give her a moment to compose herself. As he stared at the pictures hanging on the wall, he noticed that a lot of them had the Tate kids in them with Jeff and Melanie was absent in most of them as was Kate.

"Did your families spend a lot of time together?"

"Most of the time. Usually, the girls would come over and play with Iris."

"Sara mentioned when I spoke to her that she usually came over to spend the night with Iris alone and that it was unusual for Jenny to tag along. Would you agree with that?"

"Not really. I guess so, I just never really thought about it. When the girls were little, they both would come over, but you know how kids are when they get older. Jenny and Sara are so different, and my Iris and Sara have always been so close. I would say yes in the last year or so; Sara has been here more than Jenny, but I just assumed that was because she was home helping Melanie with Jack."

"So you didn't find it odd that Jenny was here that evening?"

"No, not really."

"Did Jenny act any differently when she was here?"

"Jenny over the last three years has become a very odd child. I think that has a lot to do with the fact that she doesn't want to be anything like her sister. I think it's just a twin thing."

"I know I'm kind of jumping around a bit, but I wanted to know since you and Melanie were so close, did she confide in you anything about her marriage?"

"Nothing."

"She never talked to you about her marriage?"

"She did, but anything I tell you is going to be taken out of context and make Jeff look bad, and Jeff didn't do anything to his wife."

"I'll be honest with you Ms. Murphy. The husbands are always a suspect. Do I think he did something?" Yates shrugged his answer. "I do think that something fishy is going on here and the only way to help your friend and bring her home to her kids and her friends, is for me to know as much as I can. You have information that I need, and I need your help."

"Melanie suspected Jeff of cheating on her on multiple occasions.

She never had any evidence of it, just a lot of suspicions. They argued over her money all the time. I think it was just because he was mad she went behind his back and set up the trust for the kids."

Yates made a note to take a closer look at Melanie's financial records as well when he got back to the office.

Kate continued, "He was livid when she set up that trust. I understand why she did it. Jeff is irresponsible when it comes to money. Melanie's kids are her life, and all she has ever wanted was to secure their future. She never wanted that inheritance, but since she had it, she was going to put it to good use. I just never understood why he wanted access to it so badly. It's not like they were broke. He has a good job, as far as I know they had no real substantial debt. They had the life everyone wanted. On the outside, they were perfect."

"Do you think someone could have been jealous of such perfection?"

"No," she said shaking her head, "Not anyone we knew at least. We've all lived with each other forever. We all know everyone's business. Everyone knew my husband was cheating on me before I did. It was Melanie who had the courage to tell me."

Detective Yates got up and walked around the office to get a better look at the pictures when he noticed an older girl in some of them.

"Is the other girl your daughter?"

"Yes, that's my daughter Lily."

"How old is Lily?"

"She's 17."

"Was she here the night the girl's stayed over?"

"No, she lives with her father."

"Oh, so Iris is not your Ex's child?"

"No, she is. Lily had some behavioral problems, and I thought it was best if she stayed with her father for a while. If you'll forgive me, Detective, I have to pick Iris up from school", Kate said motioning toward the door.

Yates took the hint and followed her out. "I have just one more question if you don't mind?'

"No, go right ahead."

"How long has Lily been with her father?"

"She's been there about a month."

"Thank you, Ms. Murphy. I appreciate all the information you've given me and your time", Yates said as he dodged the rain back to his car.

The trip back to the office was slow going. The Interstate was always a mess at that time of day, and the rain didn't help matters at all. Yates took every back road he could think of to get back to the station where he started the agonizing process of looking over their financial statements.

His office was bare bones; some would consider it minimalist. The only thing he had on his desk beside paperwork and a laptop was a World's Greatest Husband coffee mug that was so old he often wondered if the title still fit. The coffee inside it, so ancient it now had a dead fly bobbing on the surface. He scrunched his nose at it and pulled down the first stack of papers, Jeff's financials.

There wasn't anything of note on the first few pages until he made it to the end, one large withdrawal about a month ago that then went into a savings account. The money seems to have just stayed there. He thought it was curious that he withdrew $50,000 from his checking account and then seemed to have moved it to a savings account a few days later. Yates pulled the records for that account and the money, still there with a bit of interest accrued.

The significantly smaller stack was Melanie's records. Kate was right in the sense that Melanie seemed to be very frugal with her money. There were very few transactions outside of the normal expenses. Then he saw it, two months ago a check for $10,000 and as he went back, he saw quite a few checks, every two weeks like clockwork he saw a recurring payment of $4,000. He sent an email to his assistant to get him copies of those checks. It seemed that Melanie was using her substantial inheritance for something but what he didn't yet know.

16

Brian spent about forty-five minutes each day commuting to work.

During that time, he lamented the state of the Union, his inability

to understand why people can't use a turn signal and his ever

increasing age. He turned the radio on to Big 100, the D.C. area's

classic rock station, to calm his nerves as he attempted to navigate

the traffic around the Mixing Bowl. When *December* by Collective

Soul came on he sang along and muttered to himself, "Collective

Soul should not be on a classic rock station." They were a 90's

band, and he had spent his teen years listening to them, but that

was 20 years ago. The realization of that fact depressed him; his

rumination cut short when his favorite song came on the radio.

He turned the volume up and started to sing along to, *Stuck in the*

Middle. He mimicked as best he could sitting in the driver's seat

the dance Mr. Blonde did in *Reservoir Dogs*. He imagined Jeff as the cop, as he was all too eager to pull his ear off. Freddy wouldn't shoot him either; he would get the gratification of being able to burn the jerk alive. His daydream quickly interrupted by the driver next to him who smiled when their eyes met. Brian's cheeks flushed immediately with the realization that she was watching him dance in his seat. He gave her a quick wink before changing lanes so he could take the next exit that would lead him to Melanie's neighborhood.

Her house on Lake Tree Drive was the embodiment of the American Dream. The large front and back yard had access to a trail that ran through what was deemed as one of the most beautiful parks in the Country. On many nights, he sat and watched them from the trail; he imagined himself living that beautiful life with her. It was everything that he could want in life, a beautiful wife, and wonderful kids. All they needed was a dog. A travesty he would surely remedy as soon as possible. A big dog, like a Husky, no a Golden Retriever, those were the typical family dogs. He had never owned a pet before; his mother always told him the apartment complex they lived in wouldn't allow pets. He figured it was probably just a lie she told him because she didn't want one. One of many lies his mother told him. She was gone now, her lies no longer mattered.

He was curious to see how many reporters were still around. It was a sad state of affairs that after a week, the street was pretty much dead except for one lone news van that appeared to have just finished up a quick update report for before packing it in and leaving. "That's how fast they forget about you," he mumbled to himself.

He would never forget the first night he saw her. The big picture windows that made up the back of the house gave him an unobstructed view of the kitchen, dining and family rooms. He was grateful that all the formal rooms were in the front of the house and hardly ever used. He watched Melanie at the sink with Jack in a Moby wrap. Every so often she would stop putting away dishes to kiss Jack on the head. He watched Sara twirl around the family room to some silent song as Jenny sat at the kitchen table drawing a portrait of her mother. The beauty of it at times overwhelmed him, and he would cry, he longed to be there, beside them.

Brian made the right out of her neighborhood and got back to the main street and headed home. The first part of his plan, he executed flawlessly, Brian only hoped the rest would go as smoothly. The house was quiet upon entry as he expected it would be. He imagined coming home to the chaos of a home as other husbands did. He thought about how people take that stuff for granted. The silence was his enemy; he hated it. He spent too many days surrounded by its emptiness.

He walked down the hall to the back of the house where the door led down to the room where he kept Brie. He pushed the bell and went back upstairs to grab their dinner. Brie pulled off her nightgown and put on the dress that Brian had laid out for her that morning. It was a pale pink and fit her perfectly. She tried not to think about the fact that everything he bought for her was her exact size, right down to her shoes. The more she thought about it, the less random it all became and that thought terrified her.

The locks began to click, and the heavy door creaked open as Brian walked in with their dinner.

Proud of himself, he said, "I made beef stew in the crock pot. I hope it's edible."

He set up the TV tray in front her with a bowl of stew and some dinner rolls. He then took off his suit jacket and sat it on the footboard of the bed. Brie noticed a pen in the pocket of his jacket and tried to figure out a way to get it without him noticing. Brie quickly finished her stew; she was starving having only had trail mix and fruit to get her through the day.

"Can I have some more?"

"Really, it was that good?"

"Yes, it was, and I'm very hungry. I could eat just a bit more."

Brian happily went back upstairs to get more. While he was out of the room, Brie leaned over and tried to grab the pen but it was too far away from her reach, he had left the door open, and she was sure he would hear the chain scraping the floor. She leaned over, picked up as much of it as she could of the chain and holding it over her head with one hand; she lifted her chained foot up onto the bed. Brie scooted closer to the jacket, reached and grabbed the pen. Then she moved back into her previous position as quietly as possible and leaned over to her pillow sticking the pen far into her pillowcase. It was then that she remembered there were cameras in the room and wondered if perhaps he was watching her the whole time. Nervously, she awaited his return.

Brian reentered the room, "Here's your stew. You know if you're hungry during the day maybe I could bring a small fridge down here, and I could fill it with some things for you."

Brie ate her stew and waited for him to say something about the pen or at the very least check his jacket, but he didn't. She thought it was safe to assume that he wasn't watching. When she finished her second bowl, he told her to get a shower while he cleaned up. Brie walked into the bathroom with her pajamas and closed the door as far as the chain would allow.

Brian gathered up everything and returned upstairs. Once Brie had finished, she began to look for a new hiding place for her pen. She was free to move about the room now; he expected it. Brie grabbed the pen from inside her pillow case and rolled it under the tiny dresser. It was far enough under that you couldn't see it but close enough that she would still be able to grab it if she laid down on the floor and stuck her hand underneath.

Brian came down, to say a quick goodnight and turned off all the lights before locking her back in again. Brie laid in bed willing herself to fall asleep. Tomorrow she would write a note, slip it inside one of the library books Brian had left for her to read and pray that someone saw it when he returned it.

Upstairs, Brian paced around in his bedroom. He couldn't sleep. Insomnia had taken hold of him years ago, and he used his restlessness to his advantage. He could stay awake long after the family he watched was in bed. He remembered one particular evening after everyone had gone to sleep, he walked around in their back yard. As he sat on the red chaise lounge chair on the patio, he found a long brown stray hair that he was sure belonged to Melanie. He grabbed it and drove one-handed the entire way home clenched it in his right fist so he wouldn't lose it. He still had that lone hair, tucked away in a white envelope.

He rifled through the items on his desk; he needed to make sure he still had it. Brian said to no one in particular, "Where is it, where is it? Damn it, did I lose it?" He pushed aside papers, notes, and folders that contained pictures of Melanie and her family until finally there it was. He breathed a sigh of relief when he found it, holding it close to his chest and breathing a quick sigh of relief. He didn't dare open it and risk the contents falling out. It was enough to know it was in there just on the inside, waiting for him.

17

Jeff remarked to the gas station cashier, "Beautiful day," as he waited for her to bag up his bottle of water and breakfast sandwich. She gave him an odd look in reply; she had obviously seen him on the news. It was like he couldn't enjoy a nice day just because his wife was missing. It was ridiculous; he still had to live. He wished he could announce to the world that it didn't stop turning just because Melanie was missing. He still had kids to take care of; he still had needs. He rolled his eyes at the clerk before grabbing his bag and walking back to his car.

Autumn had arrived. The sky was a mix of orange, brown and red leaves as each casual breeze blew more away, with the occasional pre-winter gust blowing through and stirring up the ones that had already fallen to the ground. It was brisk, and that was exactly how Jeff liked it. The cool mornings that gave way to warmer afternoons. He liked the unpredictable in-between time that was the change of seasons. He sat in his car watching the leaves fall for what seemed like forever to him, eating his sandwich, when he saw her car pull up. "God, she's gorgeous," Jeff said aloud as he watched as she parked way over on the far side of the lot, he wondered if she saw his car or if she did it on purpose. She walked into the store and a few minutes later came out with a bag of her own and then walked over to his car and got in on the passenger side.

He leaned over the console and gave her a kiss. He wanted her. It didn't matter that is was the back seat of his tiny Prius, broad daylight, he didn't care. It's not like they never did that before. It was all that backseat time that had gotten him into the pickle he was in now, but he didn't care. She wanted him, desired him, and that was all he wanted. Being wanted by her or anyone for that matter made him feel alive again. The life of a father, husband, and employee was too draining and predictable. Jeff didn't care that she was only 17, she knew her mind. Some girls are just mature for their age, and Lily was very mature.

Admiring her figure, Jeff said, "You're glowing, you look gorgeous this morning."

Lily blushed and looked away. He could tell she was worried about something.

"What's on your mind?"

"What did you do? My mom is worried."

Jeff shook his head, "Why would you think I would do anything? Wouldn't that be the complete opposite of what we're trying to do?"

"I guess," Lily said lowering her head letting her long blonde hair fall, hiding her face. "I just figured, y'all argued or something and it was an accident."

"We didn't argue; she didn't know. Your mother handled everything; it was going as planned. This is just some odd coincidence."

"So, what are we gonna do now?"

"We have to wait; you'll have to go back to your father's and stay there. If the police catch me with you, that's it. You're still underage, Lily. If they don't arrest me for Melanie, they'll surely

arrest me for this", he said placing his hand on her stomach.

18

It was the beginning of October; it was also the time of year that Yates hated most. During the summer, you expected the area to become inundated with tourists. Living in such proximity to the Nation's Capital came with a few mild irritations, the first and the last being the tourists. He was sure New York City had to be worse, but he had never been. Traffic in the summer on a Friday afternoon pretty much brought the whole region to screeching halt. But October brought what Yates called, "Leafers" to the area. It didn't matter what day of the week it was, until those damn leaves fell off the trees, good luck getting anywhere.

Early in the morning, before the buzzing of his cell phone woke him up, Yates went over the case in his mind hoping for a break. The call informed him that a woman's purse was found off the trail in Burke Lake Park about three miles away from the Tate house. He asked for the area to be roped off and hoped he could convince

Alvarez to have the park shut down so they could do a full search. It was tourist season, and he had huge doubts that he was going to get permission to have all 888 acres of beautiful leaves closed to the public.

"Nice day for a walk in the park," Yates said as he followed the Officer down to where the jogger had found the purse and called it in. The jogger sat on the gravel trail and got up briefly to shake the Detective's hand before watching him walk off the trail and into the trees where he saw the tan purse. Yates took a pair of latex gloves from his pocket and put them on. Walking carefully and looking around him with each step he took until he arrived at the purse. I hope I can get up from this, he thought as he squatted down over the purse and opened it up. Inside he saw car keys, a wallet, a packet of baby wipes, a few snack size bags of Goldfish, and a prescription bottle in the name of Melanie Tate. They had found her purse. He was just about to go back up to the trail to talk to the jogger when he saw Detective Alvarez standing at the top of the slope.

Alvarez yelled from the top, "We need to talk."

Yates walked up and asked for a minute so he could talk to the jogger so he could let him go. The jogger, Steve Hester was in his mid-forties and dressed in the stereotypical jogger attire. Steve took the trail every morning but on this particular morning, his running shoe untied, and when he stopped to lace it back up, he saw it.

"I saw something brown out the corner of my eye, didn't look right. I walked up to it and saw it was a purse. You don't see much trash around here, and I knew that woman was missing, so I figured I should call the police."

"Thanks, Steve. Did you see anything else?"

"Not really, at least, nothing that strikes me as odd, you know?"

Yates gave him his card and took his information, then sent him on his way.

"You know I need to get in here with some officers and tear this park apart. Drag the lake too."

Alvarez shook his head, "Do you have any reason to believe she's in the lake? You always want to jump the gun. You know the

Captain is not going to give you divers to search that lake when you don't have one piece of evidence that says she's in the lake."

Yates knew he was right; the Captain wasn't going to spend one cent of the budget on divers right now. He would need a blood trail leading from the purse through the woods and to the lake to get that. There was obviously a link between the house and the woods even though her abduction took place, across town at the Wal-Mart. He needed to get into those woods and search, but if he couldn't convince Alvarez, he wasn't going to convince their Captain.

Yates rubbed his temple and said, "I got her purse, dumped right here."

"Yeah and it was dumped how many miles from the house?"

Yates scratched his head, "About 2-3 miles up the trail from here."

"Exactly, I share your suspicions but without something concrete that screams, hey we need to search this park from top to bottom, Captain's not giving the men or the hours."

"I know."

"Don't even try to do it yourself."

"I know."

Walking back to Yates' car, Alvarez said, "The real reason I came all the way up here was to give you some information that might be useful."

"What's up?"

"You remember that John Doe I was working on, the one from the night Tate disappeared?"

"Yeah."

"He ain't a John Doe no more. He's Michael Thomas Neill."

"Ok, so why was his body in a dumpster behind the Whole Foods?"

"Don't know that yet. But I did track down his phone records, and I think you're going to want to take a look at them."

"Why's that?"

"There were two familiar numbers that turned up."

"Whose?"

"Jeff Tate's and Kate Murphy's"

"So who is this Mike Neill?"

"He was locked up in Cooley the same period that Melanie worked there."

"So what's Jeff doing talking to an ex-con?"

19

Jenny yelled as loud as her voice would let her, "Daddy!"

Jeff came running down the hallway expecting to see blood, a

broken bone or something that would have warranted such a loud

outburst so early in the morning.

"What's happened?"

Jenny motioning to the window said, "The news vans are back.

Did they find mom?"

"No one's called me," Jeff said looking out the window at the vans

that were now lining the street. He debated briefly if he should

keep the girls home or just suck it up and venture outside. Daring

to go outside, meant dealing with all the accusations and sideways

glances that he received on a daily basis. His co-workers had

become so uncomfortable with his presence that they nicely asked

him to work from home. His manager made it seem like he was

doing him a favor but they both knew what was going on, Jeff's comfort was the least of their worries.

As Jeff looked down onto the street below from the peeled back curtain, he knew that something had happened, but he figured it was safe to assume that since the cops were not out front, they weren't going to arrest him today. Did he think, maybe they found her body? Wouldn't someone have called before the media found out? That could be a lawsuit; he could sue the City.

Sara drifted into the room carrying Jack, "What's going on? You woke up Jack."

"There are news vans outside," Jenny said to her sister and motioned for her to come and take a look.

"Yeah, they found some evidence over in the park. I heard it on the radio, this morning."

Jeff said annoyed, "Why didn't you come and wake me up? You should have told me, Sara."

Sara handed Jack over to Jeff and walked out saying, "Why would I wake you up to tell you something you already knew?"

Jeff shook his head and told Jenny to get ready for school. He tried calling Yates but got his voicemail. He didn't bother leaving a message. He figured he would hear from him soon anyway. He went through the motions of getting the kids ready for school, and Jack fed before it was time for them to head out and face the world.

The press was all over them as soon as the front door opened. They yelled out question after question to Jeff, and he just ignored them. He piled the kids in the car and drove over to the high school to drop off Sara and Jenny. From there, it was a short three blocks to his mother's house where he would drop off Jack before heading back home to work. Today, of all days he was grateful he didn't have to go into the office. Everyone either stared at him for some giveaway that he was a murderer or gave him the "puppy dog, I feel sorry for you" face. He didn't know which was worse.

****

Sara and Jenny parted ways almost immediately upon entering school. Sara's friends were usually all hanging out in the rear of the school. Laura Gardner was Jenny's only close friend, and it seemed ever since her mother disappeared, Laura avoided Jenny like the plague.

Jenny waited that morning in front of Laura's locker before homeroom. She hadn't had anything more than a "Hi/Bye" conversation with her in weeks.

Jenny yelled to Laura when she saw her, "Hi."

"Hey."

"Can I ask you something?"

Laura started putting her sweater and books into her locker, "Sure."

"Are we still even friends?"

Laura stopped, Jenny was her best friend in the whole world, and it made her sad that she was asking her that. Instead of relaying all that, she just said, "Yeah, why?"

"Cause I've called and texted and I even Facetimed you and nothing. Did your mom say you couldn't talk to me or something cause I thought she thought I was cool."

"No, it's nothing like that."

"Then what's up?"

Laura looked around, most of the kids were already in homeroom, and the halls were beginning to clear. She grabbed Jenny's arm and pulled her down the hallway toward the library. It was the one place they could be in the morning instead of homeroom without getting a demerit; they could talk there as long as they were quiet.

Jenny was intrigued, Laura was never this dramatic. They walked between the stacks and Laura whispered, "I'm scared."

"Why are you scared?"

"I'm afraid your Dad is going to kill me."

The words hit Jenny harder than a punch to the gut; she couldn't believe what she had just heard. She stared at her friend in disbelief before saying a little too loud, "What the hell, Laura."

"Shhh," her friend reminded her and looked around to see if the librarian was coming.

"Okay," Jenny said, her voice just above a whisper, "Why do you think my dad is going to kill you?"

Laura was so nervous she began to ramble, "I know things about him, and I'm scared the cops are going to come and ask me. If they ask me, then I'm going to have to tell them, I can't lie to the Police. Then your Dad is going to try and kill me and then I'm going to have to go into witness protection and leave my friends and what if my Mom and Dad don't want to come then I'm going to have to get adopted by some strange family and what if..."

Jenny stopped her friend who was about to have an anxiety attack right there in the library. Laura not only had an active imagination but was always worrying about stupid things. Jenny's job as her friend was to tell her to calm down and that it was nothing for her to worry about. She remembered last summer when she and Laura went to sleep away camp and for the entire last month of school, she had a stomach ache because she was afraid to go. Laura sincerely believed that Jenny's Dad was going to kill her, but why?

Jenny hugged her friend and said, "Just calm down Laura, my Dad wouldn't harm anyone. He didn't even do anything to my Mom. Someone took her for her money, and they'll ask my Dad for it, and we'll get her back. When that happens, she'll come home, so don't worry."

"But you don't know."

"Then just tell me."

"You remember when we went to the mall, and I had all that money to buy my Winter Dance dress?"

"Yeah."

"I got the money from your Dad."

"My Dad gave you $300?"

"Yeah."

"Why would he give you $300?"

"At first, he didn't give me $300. He gave $50, then after your mom had disappeared he called me and gave me another $250."

Jenny was scared to ask this question, but she knew she needed to ask it, "Why?"

Laura looked around then leaned in and whispered into Jenny's ear, "I'm the only one who knows your Dad wasn't at home the night your Mom disappeared. He called me and asked me to babysit Jack."

Jenny felt the room spinning; her Dad needed an alibi but not this one. If he wasn't at home then where was he? Jenny felt her legs go out from under her, and she slid down to the floor. Under normal circumstances, she loved the library, but the smell of the books made her nauseous. She felt like the stacks were closing in on her, she had to get out of there. Unsteady, she stood up and ran to the bathroom down the hall to throw up. She dry heaved multiple times before finally resting her head on the cool porcelain, her tears like tiny rain showers falling into the bowl.

20

Brian said aloud to his reflection, "I will not think about Beth today. I will not think about Beth today. That bitch can rot in hell".

Brian stared into the mirror in his bathroom. He had dreamt about Beth last night. Ten years later and he still thought about her, she haunted him. He couldn't help himself. He was still in love with her. His reflection taunted him, "Past tense, loved her. You can't love someone who's not there. But you could still want them, be desirous of their presence even after every wrong, they would still be there, the leech in your brain determined to blot out all happiness".

He tried to focus on Brie; he had taken the day off from work to spend the day with her. He couldn't deal with a job today, not today. He wanted to create something beautiful with Brie to blot out the anger he still felt. Sometimes he wished he could dig her up and kill her again; she deserved it. If there were a God, He would have sentenced her to an afterlife of being repeatedly killed by him.

He didn't want to think about it, but until he let his mind wander, the memory would haunt him. He would keep having the dreams no matter how hard he tried to let it all go. Her ghost required it of him. Every year, it was the same thing. Every year, he resisted the urge to do it again. There were times he failed, some poor chick looked a little too much like Beth, and she got it, just like she had. He would resist the urge today. He loved Brie, and she was going to give him back the family that Beth took away.

He sat down on the bed, composed himself then made his way downstairs.

The days ticked by quicker than Brie thought it ever could. She tried to keep track but the monotony of her days soon ran into one another. It was easy to lose track. Each night when Brian returned from work they played a board game. They had fun together despite their relationship being captor/captive. Brie repeatedly reminded herself that she was not on vacation and that she was held here against her will. Inside she felt a sort of friendship towards him, if they weren't in this situation she could be friends with him. However, she was in this situation and not seeing her kids for so long had made her incredibly depressed. Brian thought it was from lack of contact so he bought her a Surface so she could entertain herself. He rigged it pretty well. She could only email him. All the other emails she sent bounced back. She could only get on Netflix if she wanted to watch TV. She tried once to use Internet Explorer and log into her email only to find it blocked.

Brian had positioned himself to be her entire world. He controlled her communications and her entertainment. The little bit of control she thought she had resided in the fact that she could pick what she wanted to watch. With every day that passed, she had mixed feelings about Jeff. She loved him but the years of life that fall within a marriage had corroded it. He was not the man she thought he would be as she was positive she had not grown into the woman he thought she would. Despite it all, she held it together. She couldn't imagine her life without him and yet she was living it now.

She was in the midst of watching *The House of Yes* when Brian opened the door.

"Good morning, I'm sorry I'm so late with breakfast," he said setting down her tray, "I took off today from work and slept in a little."

She began to dig in, "That's fine."

Brian watched her eat and said, "I wanted to spend some time with you, but I need to step out for a bit and run some errands, is there anything you would like?"

She thought about it for a minute. Brie would have asked for some new books, but she hadn't had a chance to write the note yet. She didn't want to let on that she finished reading them until she had written the note.

"Could I have my purse? It has pictures of my children in there, and I'd like to have it."

"I got rid of it."

She hung her head and continued to eat not saying anything else. Brian wanted to make her happy today of all days. He knew he would have no peace today, but it could give it to someone else.

"I have an idea. What if you could have anything from home to remember your children by until we could become a family, what would you want?"

"Jack's baby blanket and something of Jenny's and Sara's."

"Done."

He sat with her until she was done her breakfast, then he cleaned up and left as usual. She doubted he would ever come by those items, and if he broke into her house to get them, she was sure he would be arrested. Brie began to imagine him throwing a rock against the window the alarms sounding, the Police circling and arresting him. They would drag him in and interrogate him. He'd break and confess to everything. They would find her; she would go home.

Brian waited until 10 am before he left, he had learned Jeff's new routine by now. During the day, while the girls were in school he worked out of his mother's house. He spent some time with Jack but mostly he worked and stayed on the phone. Brian drove past their street two blocks, parked outside of a house that was for sale and grabbed a backpack from out of his trunk. Now on foot, he walked down the street to the road that would lead to the house. There was a trail that cut just behind the property, and he would walk that, entering through the back door in case there were any police officers that canvassed the area.

Once at the house, Brian quickly sprinted through the yard and up to the back door. He took out the key he had made, opened the door and put in the code 5409 into the security system. He gently closed the door behind him. The house was quiet. The signs that a woman was no longer there was evident. The house was a mess. Dirty dishes lingered in the sink far longer than they should have. Take out boxes and plastic utensils lined the counter tops. As he made his way up to the bedrooms, he stepped over the laundry strewn about the floor. It made him angry that Jeff was not taking care of things the way he should have. It was like he didn't care at all. He knew he didn't care at all.

He had been in this house before, walked the halls when no one was home. He knew exactly where her perfume was; he sprayed a little into the air hoping that when Jeff came home, the smell of her in the house would freak him out. He sprayed it on the pillow cases and down the hall before sitting it back on the white antique vanity table and wiping it of any fingerprints. He left the master bedroom and walked down the hallway to Sara's room. He loved her bedroom; it was perfectly pink and exactly what he thought a young girl's room should be. He opened up the double doors to her walk in closet and began rummaging through the piles of clothes. Sara had the wardrobe of a Hollywood movie star; to say she was spoiled would be an understatement. Brian was looking forward to the day when he could spoil her, even more, when they were a family. There in the back of her closet, hanging up neatly were an array of scarves. He took a hot pink paisley printed one that he saw her in on more than one occasion.

Jack's nursery was sandwiched between the two largest bedrooms. You could tell by the décor that it had originally been a guest room that quickly turned over to a nursery. The walls were a neutral cream with circus animal stickers on the walls. Brian felt sorriest for Jack; he knew the little guy could not understand where his mother was; he just wanted her back. He leaned over the crib and smiled at the tiny stuffed bear that sat in the corner. He had left that bear there on one of his many excursions into the house. He wondered if they had even noticed it at all. He grabbed the blue blanket folded over the edge of his crib and left for Jenny's room.

Jenny's room reminded him of his room as a teenager. The walls were dark and covered with her artwork. She's an excellent cartoonist; he thought as he flipped through her work. He had artistic hopes as well at her age but like most artists; he found something practical to do with his life. He went into the military and then after his discharge; he got a desk job at a technology firm. He stood there, in front of her art desk and rifled through a few of her drawings, finally grabbing the one that looked like Brie. It was the detail of her hair that struck him the most. How it seemed like it had almost come to life on the page. He could almost feel the breeze blowing as he looked at it. He grabbed an empty folder from the top of her desk and placed the drawing inside to keep it from getting bent in his backpack. As he began to make his way to the back of the house, he heard the creak of the front door.

Brian stood perfectly still and held his breath waiting to hear who was at the bottom of the stairs. He hadn't lingered in the house that long, barely ten minutes had passed. It was then he heard Jeff's voice on his cell phone talking to someone about meeting up. He could hear him coming up the front steps; Brian quickly made his way to the back staircase that let out into the kitchen. By the time, Jeff reached the top of the landing; Brian was in the kitchen and going out the back door. He raced down the hill in the backyard to the trail that would eventually take him back to his car.

"Nothing like a little excitement," Brian said to no one in particular as he drove down Route 1 away from the Tate house.

It was starting to drizzle and the way the sky was becoming increasingly darker, Brian knew it was going to pour any minute. That's when he saw her, Beth. She could have been Beth's clone, standing in the rain at the bus stop all alone. For the time of day, the area was unusually deserted. The woman, in her early twenties, stood in the corner of the bus overhang trying desperately to keep warm and dry, she was failing at both. Brian fought with himself; the urge to stop was too strong like gravity pulling his body toward hers. He pulled his car into the bus parking lane and rolled down his window.

"Hi," He yelled at the woman out of the window, "Would you like a ride? It looks like the weather is going to get worse."

The woman thought about it for a second; she knew she shouldn't get into a strange person's car, especially a man. She was running late for work and had just missed the last bus; it would be another twenty-five minutes before the next one came. She had just started her job as a waitress and could not afford to be late again. Against her better judgment, she walked over to the car and looked in the window. He seemed unassuming enough, so she agreed.

"The back seat if you don't mind, I have a bunch of junk in the front."

The back seat suited her just fine, just like taking a taxi. She thought, "There's no way he could hurt me if I'm in the back seat."

"Where are you headed?"

"I work at Pete's Bar and Grill in Springfield; you don't mind do ya?"

"That's ways away, but it's fine, I have no place to be right now. Do you mind if I take the highway, we'll get there quicker?"

"Nope, that's fine."

Brian drove toward the entrance ramp to the Interstate as she rambled on in the backseat about her boss.

"I'm Gretchen by the way," she said as she extended her tiny cold hand towards the front seat. Brian reached back with his right hand and quickly grabbed hers to shake.

"Henry."

"Thanks so much Henry for giving me a ride, you're my knight in shining armor," Gretchen said with a slight giggle. It was then that she noticed they were going the wrong way. How could she not have noticed it before? She must have been too busy chatting him up to see it. "We're going the wrong way?"

"I know."

Gretchen started to panic; she looked over at the door handle, but there was no way to unlock the door from the back seat. She desperately pulled on the door handle anyway, but it would not budge.

"Just pull over and let me out."

"No."

She started to fumble through her purse for her cell phone, Brian looking through the rear view mirror watched her and then leaned over and grabbed his gun from out of the glove box.

"Do you see this," he said holding up the gun.

"Yes," she said now hysterical.

"Throw your cell phone into the front seat."

She did as she requested.

Brian hated guns; he had no intention of using it on her. Guns were too cold, too distant. When he finally did kill her, he wanted to be close to her. He had to be able to feel her, the release as she died in his arms, it was the only way. He drove west for another thirty minutes until they reached her final destination.

21

Jenny and Sara sat separately on the bus home. Jenny, usually

behind Sara and her friends, sat drawing caricatures of them. They

never had to ride the bus before their mother disappeared. She had

always done the pickups and drop-offs, she was never late. Sara

relished in her new found notoriety, but Jenny hoped that their

fifteen minutes would fizzle out sooner rather than later.

Sara led the charge back to the house from their bus drop off point

about three houses down. It was still a bit warm for mid-November

and with their mother not around Sara could get away with

wearing whatever she wanted to school. Today, it was a pink plaid

pleated skirt that fluttered in the breeze as she ran up to the front

steps. They figured it would be their Grandmother Rose greeting

them at the door but instead they saw their father. Their

Grandmother would be over soon to watch them because he had a meeting.

Sara went straight up to her room and closed the door while Jenny started to clean up the house in an attempt to spend some time with her Dad.

"Dad," Jenny said as she began washing the mound of dishes that piled up in the sink, "Do you think we'll ever know what happened to Mom?"

"I don't know," he said annoyed. He did not want to have this conversation now. He was tired of it, tired of the stares from strangers and neighbors alike. Tired of taking care of kids he didn't want. Melanie wanted to have a family, not him and now he was stuck with them. He couldn't push them all off on his mother; that wouldn't be fair. Jeff didn't have the excuse of not being able to take care of a baby with the older two; he had to be their father even when he didn't want to be.

"I just wondered because it's been so long and I miss Mom," Jenny said allowing only one tear to roll down her cheek before she caught control of herself.

"Where is my mother," Jeff wondered aloud, half asking and half just making a statement so he could get out of there as soon as possible.

It wasn't too long after that he heard the familiar giggle of Jack and his mother's voice as they walked in the front door. Jeff quickly said his goodbyes to the girls and told his mother he would be late tonight. Rose said nothing and walked around the house picking up the discarded take-out containers and other trash he had just left behind.

While Sara lay in her room with her cell phone attached to her ear, Jenny assisted her Grandmother with Jack and making dinner. She had always been close to Rose; Jenny enjoyed it when she would let her braid and play with her hair. Jenny remembered as a child that she had long black hair that she would play in and as her Grandmother got older, she cut her hair into the bob she had now. It wasn't much for braiding, but as they sat in the kitchen waiting for the oven to heat up, she could still run her fingers through it.

"Grandma Rose. Can I ask you something?"

"Anything you want Jenny," she said as Jenny ran her fingers through her hair.

"Do you think Dad misses Mom?"

"I'm sure he does."

"Is that why he acts the way he does?"

"How does he act?"

"Like he wishes we weren't here. We used to talk all the time. Sara was Mom's, and I was Dad's. Now he barely looks at me."

"Your Father loves all of you, Jenny. He's just under a lot of stress right now, and he's not handling it well. You have to be patient with him. He may be your Father but he's still a person and people make mistakes," Rose said putting the roast in the oven.

"Do you think he made a mistake, and that's why Mom is gone?"

"No. Jenny, your Mom is gone because someone took her."

"I'm just scared that we've lost Mom, and now we're going to lose Dad too."

"Why do you think that?"

"Because I lied when I talked to the Police and when they find out

I lied, they're going to think Dad did something to Mom," Jenny said hysterically crying.

"What did you lie about," Rose asked trying to console her.

"I heard Dad talking to you about Mom. I heard him say he wished her dead, that he wanted her gone."

"Jenny, your Father was just upset. He didn't mean it like that, and it's a good thing you didn't say anything because Detective Yates would have taken it wrong."

"I know other things too."

Rose stopped rummaging through the kitchen drawers and asked, what other things?"

"My friend Laura was here the night Mom went missing."

"What do you mean she was here?"

"Laura said Dad called her and asked her to babysit. He gave her $50 and then when Mom disappeared he called her back and gave her $250."

"I'm sorry, but your friend is lying to you. If it were true, her parents would have made her talk to the Police."

"It is true," Jenny said crying, "I saw the money. Laura is scared to death that Dad is going to kill her too. She didn't say anything to her parents; she's not going to."

Rose hugged her granddaughter and tried to calm the child down who was now sobbing in her arms, "I want you to invite Laura over to my house this weekend so we can have a talk. I'll find out what happened."

22

Brian stopped on the way back home to pick up a gift box, to put the items he took for Brie in. He had hoped that she would now finally see that he loved her so much he would take such a risk to bring her whatever she desired. He knew she wanted to be with her children and in time, he would give her that too, but right now, this was the best he could do. He carefully placed the items in the box and tied them with multiple ribbons, placing it in his trunk before heading home.

The drive took longer than normal, and Brian grew impatient. It was no longer raining out, there were no accidents, it wasn't a weekend, and yet there was traffic. He knew this was something that constantly happened, and yet here he was again murmuring to himself, "why can't people just get in their damn cars and drive, it's not that hard people." He took a deep breath in; he didn't want to go home to Brie in a bad mood. He grabbed a CD from the glove compartment and put it in, skipping over to number 5 and sat back in the driver's seat as the slow guitar began to soothe him. He began to sing along.

This was one of his favorite songs, he missed the 80's, it was a simpler time for him. He missed his childhood, the family he grew up in, he would have that feeling again. He thought about Brie as he played the drum part on his steering wheel and belted out, "I'll never let you go."

He felt his phone buzzing in his pocket, turning the volume down, he took it out; it was Brie. She had messaged him for food; she was hungry. He thought he had left her enough this morning; maybe she was tired of eating granola all day. He wished he could let her have free reign over the house, but he just couldn't trust her not to run yet. He didn't want to hurt her, but she couldn't leave, and he would do anything to keep her exactly where she was.

The air was getting chillier; fall had clearly taken hold and was about to relinquish its control to winter. Brian had promised himself that he would finish this by Christmas. He wanted to have a family for Christmas, now with Thanksgiving so close, his optimism was fading.

Brian's home resembled all the other single family homes on his street. Small, brick front with a red door and black shutters. There was an old wreath that hung on the door that was many years old. It was homemade and over time, the wind had removed some of the petals from the silk flowers that adorned it. The sun had bleached all the red roses to pale pink, and too many storms had turned all the white ones slightly yellow. It still hung on his front door welcoming no one but him to his door. That will all change soon, he thought before unlocking the door and entered the residence. Soon he would have his family again.

Brie was hoping that the footsteps she heard on the ceiling of her room were the Police. They had caught him trying to break into her house and were coming to rescue her. It was only when she heard the familiar ding of the bell, that she knew her wish was unfulfilled. She would not go home today and a sadness swept over her. Brie tried in earnest to keep the tears from flowing, but she missed her children. The little window provided just enough of a view for her to see that the leaves were changing. The holidays had to be approaching, and she would not be able to share them with Sara, Jack, and Jenny. He heart ached for them and what they must be feeling. Her body shook as she sobbed on her bed.

Brian was very proud of himself. He managed to make all Brie's favorites, and he couldn't wait to see her face when he presented her with her gift. He knew that she would be in awe of his ability to give her whatever she wanted. But when he opened the door, he saw her, lying there completely distraught and sat everything down on a nearby table before rushing over to her.

She was lovely, even when she was crying ugly tears, snot dripping from her nose. He sat beside her on the bed and ran his fingers through her hair trying to comfort her.

"Are you hurt," Brian asked concerned? Not knowing what he would do if she were. It's not like he could take her to a hospital. What would he say to them, "this is just some woman I've been keeping shackled to a radiator in my basement, make sure you give her back when you're done fixin' er up."

Brie mumbled, "I'm fine," as she stifled sobs.

Brian lifted her up by her shoulders and looked into her eyes. He stared at them, and he watched as she didn't blink just stared back in return. The whites of her eyes were red, her eyelids puffy and her cheeks were flushed. He watched as one last tear trickled down her cheek and wiped it away with his thumb. Her eyes never left his; he was so close to her now Brian could feel her chest rising and falling with each breath. He could smell the scent of the lavender bath scrub on her skin. He leaned in closer; her hair felt like silk as it trailed across his face and he inhaled deeply as Brie held her breath. He was so close now, he could feel her very essence flowing through his veins, and he desired her.

Brie sat perfectly still as she waited for him to say or do something, his lips just mere inches away from hers but she didn't move. She felt him tremble as he leaned toward her. She stared into his eyes; they looked so familiar to her that she was almost no longer afraid of him. She wasn't repulsed when he finally gave in and kissed her lips, gently at first. Then he waited. Waited for her to pull away, slap him, scream, do something but instead, she sat there and waited. He kissed her again, this time, parting her lips with his and to her surprise as well as his, she returned it. He began to kiss his way down her neck when he felt it. The tears began to roll down her cheeks and hit his face. He stopped, she would not be his, not today.

He sat back, away from her on the bed. Brie looked up at him not knowing what to do next.

"There's something on your face," she said as she noticed the red smudge on the side of it. "Are you bleeding?"

He got up and went into the bathroom and checked his face. He wiped away the remains of Gretchen with some wet toilet paper before flushing it down the toilet. "I think I cut myself shaving," he said from the bathroom as he finished cleaning up. He wet a small piece of toilet paper and stuck it to the spot where the blood was to make it look like he had only cut himself.

"I think I should leave you alone for a bit," he said as he made his way up the stairs bolting the door behind him.

Brian went up to his room and sat down on his bed and deeply exhaled and said, "What a day!" It had not gone in any way how he thought it was going to go. Best laid plans, he thought before taking the lock of brown hair out of his shirt pocket, bits of it matted together with dried blood. Grabbing an envelope off his desk, he placed the hair in it and labeled it Gretchen. He would keep it under his pillow tonight, sleeping with her one last time before she took her place with the others.

23

Jeff thought as he pulled up to Kate's house, it was starting to snow. It was just a passing shower; it was too warm actually to do anything more than that. Just the idea of winter and holidays without Melanie made him cringe. In his way, he did miss her. He missed all the things she did for him that made his life easier. The holidays were one of those things. She took care of all the gift buying, for everyone. Especially those people he didn't like, the ones he would never buy a gift for and yet Melanie was always prepared with a Yankee candle in a cute little gift bag. She made him look like the good guy so many times, more than he cared to count.

I am a good guy; Jeff thought as he looked at his reflection in the rearview mirror of his Prius, I didn't do anything wrong, it was just a passing moment of stupidity. He was prone to those moments on a regular basis. Like the first time, he cheated on Melanie. There had been multiple times, with multiple women. Most she never knew about and never would. He never could understand why he did it. Maybe it was the high he felt when someone was getting to know him for the first time. Or it might have been the constant attention but then again he doubted it because he wasn't that high maintenance. No, it was the fact that whenever he was with someone new, he got a blank slate and blank slates were nice.

He remembered Melanie, how she looked her first day of law school and how proud he was of her, jealous was more like it. She was living his dream. For those three years, they lived together he worked his way up at his advertising company and won his first Clio. To him, it meant nothing; he was just a hack who stumbled onto a few great ideas every now and again. Melanie was going places, she graduated first in her class and right out the gate got a job with one of the top Law firms in D.C. She was everything he wanted to be and never could, but it wasn't her calling, and she soon gave it up to become a social worker. They weren't married a year before she quit her job and started working in the prison. They must have fought for two years straight about it. He resented her and her happiness, so he went in search of it elsewhere.

He closed his eyes, took a deep breath before getting out of the car and banging on Kate's door.

Opening the door, Kate said, "What the hell, Jeff?"

"Just let me in," Jeff said as he walked past her and into the living room.

"Really?"

"Yes, this is what happens when you don't return my calls or my texts or my fuckin' emails."

"I don't know where he is alright."

"You need to get a hold of your cousin. Tell him I need to talk to him."

"I don't know where Mike is, and he's not my cousin. He's a friend of the family. His family grew up with mine."

"I don't care if he's your fuckin Uncle. Kate, you need to get a hold of him and tell him that he needs to meet me. I'm freaking out."

"Do you think he took her anyway?"

"What would you think?"

"I don't know what to think; you told him you changed your mind, right?"

"I told him twice I changed my mind. I told him it wouldn't work. I said that even if she were kidnapped, I wouldn't get the money. I put the money I did manage to get into a savings account."

"So, then we're fine. Why are you worrying about Mike?"

Jeff was pacing now, "Because he's not responding to my calls or my texts. What if he did something on his own? We're accessories, you idiot! I knew I should have never listened to you and your God damned cousin."

"I'm not an accessory; I didn't do anything wrong."

"You're a fucking moron. How are you not an accessory? Please, fuckin tell me how you ain't an accessory?"

"I'm not the one who was gonna pay him to kidnap my wife so I could get her money."

Jeff was livid now and ranting as he paced, "It was your fuckin idea you bitch. You went and pissed her off. You couldn't just stick to the God Damned plan. No, you had to go and tell her I knocked up Lily. All you had to do was say you needed the money for Lily to go to boarding school. Which was the original plan, I might add. She was fucking fine with that but NO, you greedy bitch, you thought you were going to get something extra on the side for yourself, so you fucked up the whole thing."

Kate was crying, "Stop yelling at me, alright."

"When she found that out her head exploded. That's why I sent the girls to your house. She was going to divorce me, and if Yates finds that out, I'm screwed, and if I'm screwed, you can best believe your ass is just as screwed."

Kate slumped on the floor in front of her white couch and laid her head back on the seat before ultimately putting her head in her hands and sobbing.

"You can't tell Yates I helped you if I go to jail who will help Lily with the baby?"

"What the fuck do I care? That kid believes I'm going to run off into the sunset with her. She's an idiot; I can't run off with a seventeen-year-old after my wife disappeared. She needs to get rid of it, is what she needs to do. I got three kids I don't fucking want already, what am I going to do with another one."

"Melanie was right about you; you grew up to be an asshole."

"I was always an asshole, princess." He turned away from her because the sight of her annoyed him.

Calmer, he thought about Melanie. The first time they met flashed through his mind, just an image of her coming into the pizza place where he worked part time during college. "Melanie was right about a lot of things, Kate. She was too good for me, and I told her so. I said it so many times I think she thought I was self-deprecating. Look, I gotta go", he said as he walked to the door and opened it, "Have Mike text me, I need to talk to him."

Kate closed the door behind him.

24

The light was already starting to fill up the room when Brie rolled

over and looked at the tiny clock on the dresser. It was well after

10 am, she didn't know how she had managed to sleep in so late.

Immediately, she panicked and sat up quickly; Brian would have

already rung the bell. She wasn't ready. She looked over at the TV

tray, breakfast and lunch were already on it. How had she slept

through the bell and the loud screech the door made every time he

opened it? She was so distraught he must have given her another

sedative. She felt a little groggy, but she couldn't remember any

drugs.

The clank of her chain hitting the floor always startled her, even

though she always knew it was coming. It was so quiet in the

basement the sound echoed loudly off the cement walls. She often

wondered if the walls were soundproofed. There was a faint smell of food when Brie lifted the lid on the plate that Brian had left for her that morning. The eggs were cold, but there was toast and bacon that she could still eat. The milk was still cold, and there was granola. It was starting to become chilly, and she wondered how cold it would get in that basement come the winter. Would she even make it to winter?

That's when she saw the box; it was sitting right on the nightstand. She didn't know how she had missed it, a pretty blue box with ribbons that had a note resting on top.

Brie,

You looked like an angel this morning; I didn't want to wake you. I hope your breakfast doesn't get too cold for you to enjoy it. I wish I could be there to see your face when you open the present I left for you. I hope you are pleased. You were so sad last night; I hate to see you that way.

Even as I write this, I can't stop thinking about yesterday. I can still feel your lips on mine. I want you to know I would never take advantage of you. Never. You know I love you. Until you feel the same way about me, I can be patient. I know deep inside there's a part of you that knows we should be together, always.

Love,

Brian

Brie thought about yesterday and closed her eyes. She could still feel his lips on hers as well. She cried because the thought excited her and she knew it was wrong. Jeff had never written her letters like that. Not even in the beginning. The longer she was away, locked in this room with all the time in the world to think, she wondered why she held on to him.

He's so good looking; she remembered thinking when he first came over to her in The Pizza Shack. She thought that it was a practical joke. Sure, she was attractive in her own right, but most people described her as cute, he was gorgeous. They were very different people, even then. He was a people person, she a classic introvert. They weren't married a year when he first cheated on her. She remembered their little kitchen; their first house could fit inside of the one they owned now. She sat there in their little kitchenette with the rooster border crying, not knowing what to do.

Melanie with tears in her eyes said, "How could you do this to me, to us?"

"I still love you, baby, I just got confused. All this being married stuff. She meant nothing to me."

"I'm sure you told her the same thing about me."

"How could you say that? You mean everything to me."

Melanie started to cry even harder when Jeff walked over and took her in his arms.

"Let me tell you something about men. Real men cheat and real women get over it. You wanna know why?"

"Why?"

"You remember that bottle of Merlot I bought you, the Bogle Vineyards?"

"Yes."

"You remember how you just loved it, drank it all the time. You must have drank like ten bottles of it."

"I remember."

"Then one day you got tired of it, I brought it home, and you said you were in the mood for something different. You still loved it, but you had drank so much of it that to drink it, literally made you wanna throw up. You remember that?"

"Yes, it did."

"So I got you a Cabernet, and you liked it but not as much as the Merlot. You even drank the shitty white from that vineyard in Harrisonville for a while, but you always went back to the Merlot."

"Okay."

"Babe, you're my Merlot. I love you, and no matter what I may go out and drink, eventually it's gonna taste like shit, and I'm gonna come back to my Merlot."

Brie had to laugh at herself for actually believing him then. She looked down at the rings on her hand and pulled them off, throwing them across the room. Melanie thought that if she ever got out of this, she was divorcing him. She wanted a better a life with someone that would respect her as much as love her.

Brie turned to open the box and pulled out, Jack's baby blanket,

Jenny's portrait, and Sara's scarf. She held each item in her hand and stared at it before smelling each one. Jack's soft blue blanket smelled like baby powder and the top of his head. Jenny's portrait smelled like a mix of oil and her patchouli scented body splash. The pink scarf smelled exactly like Sara, a mix of a summer's day and the sweetest candy you ever ate. Being able to touch these three items made her feel like they were close.

She was thinking nonsense. The only way she was going to see her kids again was if she was found. As long as she stayed locked up in Brian's dungeon, she would never go home. She had to get herself out. She walked slowly towards the bathroom, in case, Brian happened to be watching her. She slid her foot under the dresser and pulled out the pen with her toes. She walked in the bathroom, used it and when she came back out she quickly picked it up walking back over to the bed with it.

She hated to rip up a library book like this, but she had no choice, Brie grabbed one of the books and ripped out one of the blank title pages.

My name is Melanie Tate. I am still alive. I am being held in a basement by a man who calls himself Brian. I don't know where I am, but I know I am not far from my house. This is not a joke, if you get this, give it to the police.

She folded the note up several times to make it small and then stuck it in the middle of the book. Brie put it with a pile of books on the nightstand that she was going to ask Brian to return that night. Her only hope was that he wasn't watching.

25

Yates sat at his desk looking over everything again when Alvarez walked into his office.

"Anything jumping out at you?"

"Not a thing."

"You bring Jeff back in yet?"

"Nope. His lawyer is a real pain in the ass about it. Says he's cooperated enough. We either need to arrest him or leave him alone."

"Can you arrest him?"

"Nope, nothing concrete. The video clearly shows it's not him that took her, doesn't mean that he didn't hire someone. His financials don't show anything like that. Melanie's are more suspicious than his. We've been waiting for those checks to come in from her bank but it's some Podunk bank, and it's going to take them 'til next Christmas to track that down. They don't even have a website. Lucky they even have a computer."

Alvarez thumbed through the Forensic reports on Yates' desk, "What about the purse, anything?"

"Not a thing, just her prints, dirt from the area, nothing out of the ordinary."

"Maybe you should go back to the Wal-Mart or the trail, look around."

"I think, I'll try the trail again and bring a picture, maybe one of the regulars saw her or saw something."

"It's possible; maybe they saw someone hanging around or following her during one of her runs. Did you talk to the neighbors to see if anyone maybe saw someone hanging around that looked off?"

"I haven't started with the neighbors yet, pretty much kept to the Wal-Mart Lot. I put the word out that if anyone saw the car or the driver, should call it in. All I've gotten so far is a bunch of quacks."

"I'd work the financial angle until something else shakes loose. Cases like these take time; you have to be patient."

"I know. Any other news with Michael Neill?

"Nothing, just waiting for a response from Jeff's lawyer like you. As soon as I get him in, I'll let you know."

"Seems like we both got a whole lotta nothing."

"Would seem that way," Alvarez said before he punched Yates on the shoulder before leaving, "So get something."

"If only it were that easy."

****

It was a nice day to be out on the lake. Yates pulled up about mid-morning, the ground was slightly damp from the storm the day before. He began walking the trail from the Tate house down to where they found Melanie's purse. As he passed Melanie's house, he saw footprints, very faint to the point he almost missed them. He suspected they weren't fresh, maybe a day or two old and not a child size print. He followed them up the trail and they disappeared at Melanie's backyard, down the trail they led into the woods. Curiosity got the better of him, and he followed them. He was deep into the nature preserve about a ½ a mile when he happened upon a deer stand.

Yates thought, what in the hell is a deer stand doing on a nature preserve? His sixth sense was kicking in, and he just had a weird feeling about it. He checked the rungs before climbing. It was a basic stand made of old well-weathered wood. The oddest thing about it other than its location was the fact that it was perfectly empty. There should be some evidence that someone had been here at some point, but there was none. No empty beer bottles from teenagers using it as a hangout. It was too clean, and it felt off to him. He turned to look around inside and put his hand over his eyes to block the sun so he could better see what vantage point he had from the stand. That's when he saw it, a perfectly unobstructed view of the Tate house.

He called Alvarez and asked him to meet him out there, the second set of eyes on this place couldn't hurt. He climbed back down and started poking around the bottom when he heard crunching and walked back to the trail thinking it was Alvarez. That's when he saw him, standing there on the trail looking in the direction of the Tate house. He watched him as he just stood there doing nothing but looking at the house. He was about 5'11ish; his hair looked like a mix between dark blond and light brown. What made him stand out wasn't just the fact that he was staring at the house but that he was dressed like he was on his way to work and not to run a trail.

"Hey stranger," Yates called out as he jogged up to the man, "Can I trouble you a moment?"

"Sure."

"You from around here."

" I am."

"Where exactly?"

Brian pointed over in the direction of the trees and said, "Maple."

"Oh. Do you know the Tates?"

"Not really, just heard about it on the news like everyone else."

"Which house over on Maple is yours?"

Brian paused and then asked, "Why?"

"Just my curiosity, I'm a Detective, so I guess it just comes naturally."

"Number 29."

The sun went back behind the clouds, and the fall chill rolled back through again. Yates moved in closer to Brian and asked, "What brings you out here today, you sure don't seem like you're going for a hike?"

"My cat got out. One of my neighbors said she thought she saw it run this way when she tried to catch it."

"Well don't let me hold me hold you up."

Brian started to walk away, and Yates called after him, "I didn't catch your name, in case I happen across your cat while I'm out here."

"J.R. Sayers."

"What's your cat's name? In case I see it."

Brian paused for a moment and said, "Brie," before he half jogged up the trail pretending to look for his lost cat.

Alvarez walked up and caught Yates' attention.

"Who was that?"

"Some guy lives over on Maple, lost his cat. Anyway, I called you over to have a look at this deer stand out in the woods."

Yates turned and looked again, but he was gone.

"That's weird," Yates said as he ushered Alvarez off the trail and into the woods.

"What?"

"He just disappeared that quickly."

"Maybe he saw his cat?"

"Yeah, maybe. Just… Something seemed off."

"I think your radar is off," Alvarez said laughing and punched Yates in the arm.

"No, seriously. I came out of the woods, and he was just standing there looking at the Tates' yard."

Alvarez shrugged. Yates thought everyone was a suspect until he ruled them out.

Yates continued, "He said he lives over on Maple, maybe I'll swing by later, see if he found his cat."

 "Which house on Maple? Me and the wife were going to buy over there last month when we were looking at houses. They were building new ones, but they wanted too much."

"He said number 29."

"There's no number 29 Maple. There are only ten houses on that street."

Yates yelled, "Fuck it all," before running back up to the trail but he was gone.

26

Rose had just finished moving the last of her things into Jeff's house that Saturday morning. She had hoped to find some time to talk to her son. They needed to talk about quite a few things. She could see his life unraveling, and she was afraid, for him and his children.

She loved her son; she tried to raise him well. When he met Melanie, she couldn't have asked for a better daughter-in-law. All a mother wants for her son is to find love and a woman who will accept him for who he is. Melanie was always that woman. She forgave him, stuck up for him and created a wonderful family, what more could a mother want for her son? Rose continued to clean and cook at the same time when Jeff walked in, going directly to the fridge for some orange juice.

"Mom, can you stay with the kids today? I have a lot of errands to run, and I need to stick my head in the office, finish a presentation."

"Sure, but can we talk first it's really important."

"Not, now mom. I'm late as it is. We'll talk tonight, I promise. I won't get in late." He grabbed a bagel from off the kitchen island and mumbled mouth full of the bite he just took, "Tell the kids I love them," before letting the screen door slam behind him.

Jenny walked into the kitchen with Jack on her hip and Sara followed. They sat at the island and started to eat breakfast while Jack banged his toy on the highchair table.

"Jenny, did you find out if your friend Laura could come over today?"

"She can."

Sara popped up from her cell phone, "Why is Laura coming over, can I invite Iris?"

"No, not this afternoon, maybe tonight. I have to talk to Laura."

"Why?"

"Don't worry about it Sara. Just finish your food."

Jenny stopped eating and looked at Rose, "Gram, if what Laura said is true then Sara should know, she'll find out anyway."

Rose leaned over the granite island countertop and patted Jenny on the head, "You're right. Sara, Jenny's friend Laura is saying that she babysat Jack the night your mom disappeared."

Sara sat there with a look of "so what" on her face like they were giving her information she already knew.

"This is a really big deal," Jenny said waiting for her sister to give some remark.

"Iris told me that already."

Rose shocked, "How did Iris know?"

Sara said matter of fact, "Lily."

Rose asked feeling out of the loop, "Who is Lily?"

"Gram, Lily is Iris' sister. Lily is the girl Dad was seeing when our Mom went missing. I think it's disgusting because not only are we going to have a new half brother or sister but our step mom is going to be three years older than us."

Rose couldn't believe what she just heard, and she didn't know what was more shocking, the fact that her son was messing around with a seventeen-year-old child or how nonchalantly her granddaughter thinks this all is. What is going on in this house, Rose thought and immediately felt dizzy; her chest tightened with the realization that her son might be guilty of something other than bad judgment.

"Gram, are you okay," Jenny asked?

Barely catching her breath, Rose said, "Can you run in the guest room and get my medicine bag? I was so busy this morning; I forgot to take my medicine."

She felt like she was having an anxiety attack and who could blame her under these circumstances. Jenny ran upstairs and into the pale peach guest room that was once an office until Jack was born. She grabbed the small travel bag and raced back down the stairs to her Grandmother. Rose was sitting at the table. She took the pills with the glass of water Sara brought to her and then looked longingly at her cup of tea.

"Sara, where do your parents keep the whiskey?"

"It's downstairs in Dad's wine cellar."

"Can you bring it up for me?"

Sara obeyed returning with a half empty bottle of Woodford Reserve. Rose took it and poured a shot into her tea, thought about it and then poured a second shot. The warm liquid traveled slowly down her throat taking all of her fear and anxiety with it. She could breathe again. It would only be a matter of time now. She couldn't protect her son; he had made his bed, and now he was going to have to lie in it.

27

Brian looked out of his bedroom window that fine Saturday morning very pleased with himself. He walked around the house with a renewed sense of purpose. Yesterday, he was scared just a touch more than he would like to admit. That Detective, he would swear he could read his mind. He tried to keep it as blank as possible. He recited the Gettysburg Address up to the part, "Our forefathers set about to create a more perfect Union." Then he couldn't remember what came after that. He was so fixated on remembering the rest; he forgot to be nervous. Lucky for him that other Cop came and distracted him. Brian knew better than to tempt fate; he wouldn't go back to the Tate house again.

Brie laid in bed and stared at the ceiling. It was white and perfectly smooth. Usually, basements had many cracks, but this room was perfect. She searched for something to focus on, to keep her mind from remembering her old life but she couldn't. Last night, she had dreamt about this past Fourth of July and the picnic she had at the Murphy house. She loved Lily like she was her daughter. In fact, she helped Kate because she loved her kids as if they were her own. Maybe that's why the betrayal hurt so badly.

"We need to talk," Kate said as she pulled her aside in her kitchen. Melanie was watching the kids chase each other through the sprinkler Lily had helped them set up in the backyard.

"What's up?"

"I'm thinking about sending Lily away to a boarding school."

Melanie took her friend's hand, shocked and asked, "Why?"

"She's been getting into some trouble, and I think it would be best for her if she went away."

"If that's how you feel."

"I was wondering if…, you know…, you might be able to help me with the tuition, it's just too much for me, and her father is not going to help."

Melanie was surprised that she would even ask, especially after all the help she had given her in the past.

"I'm sorry, I just don't feel comfortable…"

Kate interrupted, "Look, Melanie, I didn't want to tell you this, but your husband has been coming on to my daughter, and I don't want her around him."

"What the hell are you talking about Kate, she's 17?"

"That's exactly what I'm talking about. Lily is 17, and she's dumb enough to believe all of Jeff's crap. But that's statutory rape, Melanie. You understand that. If I can't get my daughter away from him quietly, then I'm going to have to press charges."

Melanie walked away from Kate to the other side of the room, looking out of the window at the girls and Jeff, she could see him watching every move Lily made. The look on his face reminded her of the sex offenders when she worked at the prison. They looked at you like you were their next meal and they couldn't wait to eat it.

"Just let me know how much it is and I'll pay it," Melanie said as she put on her happy face and went out to the back yard holding a bowl of potato salad.

The bell rang pushing Brie out of her daydream and back to reality. She had to pull herself together before Brian came down. Brie thought, as long as she could keep him happy, she would stay alive.

She repeated this to herself so often she didn't know anymore if she was just acting or if she was becoming his. The thought scared her but not as much as she thought it should.

"You're particularly happy this morning," Brie remarked as she watched Brian walk around the small room. Each step he took looked more like a mini dance as he set up their brunch.

"I am happy, Brie."

It was unnerving to see him like that when just the other day he looked as if he were in the depths of despair.

Maybe he got his meds changed, she thought, one could only hope. She didn't even know if he was on medication or not. She supposed that someone who was willing to abduct another person and keep them in their basement should at the very least be on some sort of anti-psychotic. She stifled a chuckle; she wished she could say what was on her mind, but that wouldn't be very Brie-like, or very Melanie like.

"Today, I'm going to release you from that awful chain," Brian said dangling the keys in front of her. "Frankly, I'm tired of hearing it clank on the floor. It's getting cold, and you need to be able to dress warmer."

Brie stared at him in disbelief. The door locked from the outside and when he was in here with her, there was nothing but him in the way of her freedom. She was too weak now to even attempt to overpower him. The only freedom she would get today was the release from her chain. It had become an extension of her and a reminder that she needed to play the game. If she didn't play along, she knew first hand that it could get a lot worse than just a chain.

As Brie sat on the bed eating her toast, Brian kneeled in front of her and put her leg on his thigh. With two clicks it fell away and just like that, she was free. Out of his pocket, he pulled a small tube of lotion and smeared it on her ankle. It was red and slightly puffy. No doubt, Brie was allergic to the metal.

"I'll get that healed up in no time."

As Brian went to retrieve the rest of the chain and take it out of the room, Brie stood up. It was like she was a baby taking its first steps. She wanted to run out of the house and down the street, screaming at the top of her lungs. Running would get her nowhere but dead. She walked across the L-shaped room to the exit door. Brian had left it open when he went upstairs; she rested her hand on the railing. This was the farthest she had ever been in the room. She stood at the stairs and waited unsure of what to do next. She saw Brian pass by the door upstairs.

"Come on up; it's okay."

Brie walked to the first step scared to climb it for fear of what was at the top. She heard Brian yell out to her again.

"It is okay. I trust you."

Brie climbed the stairs and emerged into the kitchen. The walls looked white but were actually a very pale yellow. The color of which seemed to change with the direction she was facing in the room. The very detailed light blue tile floor was cold under her feet. Brie shifted from standing on her toes to flat foot. She couldn't stand her feet to be cold which was why she stayed in bed most of the day. Brian noticed how uncomfortable she was and offered her a pair of his socks.

The tiny white kitchen table she sat at looked like it had been a garage sale rescue from the 1980s. The rest of the first floor looked the same, a mix of the old and new. Nothing seemed to fit and yet the house fit Brian perfectly. It seemed like a desperate attempt to recreate a world that had long passed. Modern conveniences, like the microwave, stainless steel appliances, flat screen TV and his IPod docking station seemed out of place with the rest of the décor.

"Would you like a tour?"

Brie nodded her head and followed Brian into the living room. The walls were a pale tan, all the wood was chestnut, the tables and chair edging. It was all very formal except for the armchair that looked like a green version of the one Archie Bunker used in *All in the Family,* next to a very feminine armchair with a floral pattern Brie though was cute.

"Do you like the chair? I bought it just for you so we can sit and watch TV at night while the kids play."

Brie smiled. It wasn't her style at all. She continued to follow him up the narrow staircase to the second floor. There was only one bathroom in the hallway, small and outdated. It reminded her of an old lady's powder room, pink and white tile, pink tub, and pink sink.

"I think Sara would like this bathroom."

It was the first time he had ever mentioned the kids.

The realization of what he just said finally hit her, he's planning to take them too. She was both excited and scared by that fact.

Her mind was racing with questions of what if he did get them, what if something went wrong? What if they got hurt, would he hurt them? The other two rooms were just a blur until they got to the master bedroom.

"You can redecorate this room if you want."

She nodded in reply and continued to explore the room. It had its own very tiny bathroom off to the left and small closet. There was an old writer's desk in the corner covered with stacks of papers.

The bed was half made; the white quilt pulled up to the pillows, but the flat sheet hung off the side of the bed underneath it. As Brie walked around the bedroom and over to the desk, she heard the doors shut and lock behind her. At that moment, she knew what was coming.

Brian walked the length of the bed and over to where Brie stood at the desk. Taking her hand, he led her back to the bed and stood behind her. Every muscle in her body tensed while she waited for him to do or say something. Pulling her hair to the side, he slowly kissed the back of her neck letting his lips linger on her skin a little longer each time, waiting for her to protest. Brian raised his arms around her and began to undo the buttons down the front of her dress. Turning her to face him, he looks Brie in the eye; she's not crying like he thought she would have been. Her face gives away nothing. He pulls her dress down to her ankles, kissing every inch of her as he goes down and caressing her thighs.

"I've wanted you for so long," Brian said as he kissed the inside of her thigh before making his way between her legs.

Brie tried not to feel him, she didn't want to enjoy his touch, his kisses should disgust her but they didn't. Instead, it turned her on and when she did finally orgasm she felt disgusted, ashamed and aroused.

"Lay on the bed."

Brie quickly got onto the bed and watched as Brian undressed. Under his nerdy exterior hid a very attractive man, more muscular than she would have ever thought him to be. He laid on the bed beside her and after kissing her on the shoulder, said, "Do you want me?"

Brie didn't answer; she was afraid to say the words aloud. She didn't want to want him.

"I won't force myself on you, Brie, so if you want me, you need to tell me," he said, and he rolled on top of her covering them both with the quilt. He could see goosebumps on her skin and assumed she was cold. He kissed her chest up to her neck and Brie held her breath. When he arrived at the side of her cheek, he whispered in her ear one last time, "Do you want me?"

"Yes," she exhaled and in the same moment she felt him inside her, and the final bits of Melanie fell away.

28

This is the first Saturday in a long time that I've been able just to do me; Jeff thought as he walked into his local gym. Jeff usually spent his Saturday mornings at the gym. It was nice to work off some of his pent up aggression on the free weights. The Town of Burke Lake was big enough that not everyone knew each other but small enough that you seemed to run into everyone you knew on a daily basis. Normally, he didn't mind it, but when your wife disappears, and it's all over the news, it makes it harder running into people. The gym was the one place he could let down his guard and be free of all of it. Guys didn't care what people were saying about you. Jeff chuckled to himself, most of them secretly wished their wives would disappear on the regular.

He had met Mike Neill here once. He was running late, and Mike almost left. Jeff noted at the time how jittery and sweaty he had been. Mike was sitting over by the rock climbing wall in a simple white tee shirt, black mesh shorts, and black running shoes. He carried a small gym bag, and his brownish blonde hair was messy. Jeff hated that tousled bed head look. He had tried it once and after an hour and an entire jar of Bed Head, he looked like a hot greasy mess. He secretly envied men who could pull off the look with little effort. Mike also looked a lot younger than Jeff would have thought he would. Maybe you had to be young and dumb to be willing to risk jail for such a small amount of money.

"Random meeting place, shouldn't we have met in a parking lot somewhere?"

Mike shook his hand and said, "Too many cameras in a parking lot, there are only four in here, and right now, we're in a dead spot."

Jeff had to agree with him; he looked young and dumb, but he was smart. At least smart enough to avoid getting caught, he assumed.

"Do you have the money?"

"Yes."

"Here's the plan," Mike leaned closer to him on the bench and looked around before speaking again, "When you decide to pull the trigger on this, you give me the $50,000. I get rid of your wife and send you a ransom note. You act normal. You call the police, do what they tell you to do, get the rest of the money out of your wife's account. I'll send you an account number to wire the money to, once it hits that account it'll transfer to so many other different accounts that they'll lose track of where it's going. It will take them years to sort it all out. Once I've transferred it enough times, you and Kate will get your money into those dummy accounts I set up for you. Do not take it all out at one time and no large purchases."

Jeff sat there absorbing all the information. He knew he would forget something, but he knew better than to write it down. Mike had insisted on the use of burner phones and texting only. The texts were even in code.

Today, he had his burner phone on him, and he texted Mike again. *Meet. 9:30pm. Trail.* No response. He waited for hours, hanging around the gym long after his work out in the hopes he would randomly run into him. Eventually, people started to notice, and he left. He sat in his Prius for a long time wondering what his next move should be. It was just after 3 o'clock at this point, and he knew he had to return home. His mother had wanted to talk to him and by the look on her face, he knew not to keep her waiting.

Jeff pulled into the driveway of their house and sat there. It was the first time he was worried about his future and to some extent, the future of his family. He remembered the day he and Melanie closed on the house. It was a pretty autumn day much like it was today. Tons of leaves covered the front yard, and he laughed as Melanie fumbled to open the front door. It took a couple of tries because the lock was old and a little corroded. When she finally got it open, he scooped her up and carried her across the threshold into their new home. He could hear her laugh that sounded like a baby giggle. It was the one thing he loved most about her, that silly little laugh. It floated on the wind and then disappeared as quickly as it arrived.

The guilt weighed on him; he knew this situation was his fault. Whatever was happening or had happened to Melanie was a direct result of his actions, his stupidity, and his greed. He didn't want much, just a different life. He didn't want to be the settled down with kids guy. He enjoyed being married but the constant stress of raising a family was not what he signed on for, and he was done with it. Melanie could be so stubborn; she never gave up on him or what she wanted. She viewed divorce as a failure, and Melanie didn't fail at anything. She could never understand that there was nothing wrong with the life she wanted, he just didn't want the same thing.

Jenny tapped the glass of the Prius breaking Jeff's daydream; he rolled down the window to hear her say, "Are you okay?"

"I was just thinking about your mom; that's all." He cut the engine and walked inside taking her hand. Jenny smiled, it was the first time since their mother disappeared that he had touched her. A tear started to well up in her eye, and she quickly thought of something else to make it stop.

Jack was standing up in his play yard when Jeff entered the living and readied himself for Rose. He watched him play the familiar game of throw all my toys out of the crib and watch them fall. It amused him for some reason, and he never could figure out why.

"Jeff, can I speak with you privately when you get settled," Rose said over her shoulder when he walked in the door. Settled, pre-kids usually meant the three S's: shit, shower, and shave. Now it meant listening to whatever the kids had to say for long enough so that it would be easy to shake them off to have a grown up conversation.

After throwing all the toys back in the play yard and listening to Sara's school dramas, he was able to close off the family room to speak with his mother.

"I had a conversation with the girls this morning that was quite upsetting."

"I know they're upset about everything, Mom. I just don't know what to do about it. I have things I'm dealing with too, you know."

"What is this I hear about you and the neighbor's daughter?"

Jeff looked at Rose with the same puzzled look he gave her every time he had been caught red-handed as a child doing something he shouldn't. She hated that face, and it wouldn't work.

"Jeffrey William Tate, I'm your mother, and I know when you're trying to pull the wool over my eyes so cut the bullshit."

It was the first time he had ever heard his mother curse in the last twenty years.

"It's nothing to worry about; I have it under control."

"Is she 16?"

"She'll be 18 in a few months."

"But it started when she was 16?"

"Yes."

Rose whacked him on the side of the head, Jeff crouched and covered his face with his hands to prevent further assault. It was a pose he knew well growing up Rose.

"What the hell were you thinking?"

"It's done and over with so can we not talk about it."

"It's not done and over with. Is she pregnant?"

"Yes, and before you ask, I tried to get her to get rid of it and she won't."

Rose shook her head; her son could be a real jackass sometimes,

"Is it yours?"

"Of course, it's mine; she's not a slut, Mom."

"Any young girl who would sleep with a forty-year-old…"

"I'm thirty-eight, Mom."

"She's a child, and you should have known better. I can't believe you would do this to your marriage. You have a good thing with Melanie, a life, a good family. Why Jeffrey?"

Jeff reached over and took Rose's hand to try to comfort her.

"I don't know, maybe because I'm an idiot. I've made such a mess; you don't even know the half of it."

"I know Laura told your daughters about babysitting for you."

"What!?"

"Once she tells her parents, it's all going to unravel. Everything is going to come out."

"We need to talk to your attorney and find out what we should do."

"A lot worse is going to come out if Laura talks to her parents."

"What's that supposed to mean?" Rose was concerned, what had her son done that could be so much worse than what she already knew. She hesitated to ask, in some ways, she didn't want to know.

"Nothing, Mother. Don't worry; I'll talk to her."

"I don't think you should. I think we should call the lawyer."

"And tell him what exactly? If she doesn't say anything, then no one needs to know. I'll deal with it, Ma."

Jeff walked out of the room; he needed to think away from everyone, and his bedroom was the only place in the house he could do that. Closing his door, he sucked in a deep breath before sliding down the wall and sitting on the floor. Melanie's perfume still lingered in the air as if she had only just passed through. It was all crashing down around him, and he wondered how many more days he would have before it all fell apart.

29

Yates was going over his notes yet again when he heard the page come into the conference room. He had tried for several days to get Jeff's attorney, Mr. Berkley on the phone. He was stalling. Berkley knew he didn't have anything to charge him with, but he knew enough to know not to volunteer any more information. Yates had gotten as far as he was going to get with Jeff for the time being. He had to go another route, Kate Murphy. If there was anyone in the Tate's circle that knew more than she was telling it was her.

Kate sat dead center of the conference room table, the white walls, and the fluorescent lighting made her look pale and twenty years older, magnifying every line on her face. She had her hair pulled back in a tight bun and the black pantsuit she wore made her look overdressed for just a casual talk in a police department conference room.

She stood up when Yates walked in and shook his hand before sitting back down in her seat. The room was borderline arctic and was glad that she wore a suit jacket, but she still felt the chill.

"I should apologize about the coldness in here," Yates said noticing her shiver, "It's that time of year when the City makes us cut off the A/C, but we don't get to turn on the heat just yet. I can get you a cup of coffee to warm you up."

"That would be great."

Yates dipped out of the room for a minute and was back with two cups of worst coffee either one of them had ever tasted. Yates was used to it but upon the first sip, Kate wrinkled her nose and set it aside. She would eventually break down and drink it, being warm with indigestion was better than cold on any day.

"I'm glad you could finally come down and have a chat. There are a few things I'd like to go over."

Kate nodded her head for Yates to proceed.

"I know you said in the past Melanie has helped you with your mortgage to keep your family afloat."

"Yes, she's been very generous."

"Why?"

Kate looked back at the Detective with a puzzled look.

"The reason I ask why, Kate, is because from looking over Melanie's financial records she seemed to be a very frugal woman. I'm just curious why she would pretty much keep you afloat for years."

Yates pulled out a packet of papers with sections highlighted.

"You see here," he pointed to a chunk of highlighted transactions. "These are checks she wrote to you bi-weekly for over a year and then they stopped for a while and most recently they started back up again."

"She was helping me send my daughter to a private school. Lily had gotten into some trouble, and I thought it would be best to get her out of the neighborhood."

"She just agreed to help you, just like that?"

"Yes. I told you, Melanie was a very generous woman."

"Was?"

"She is a generous woman. She's my best friend. I came to her with a problem, and she helped me. That's the type of person she is."

"What was the trouble your daughter got into?"

"She's just boy crazy, you know she's at that age. I decided that she would be better off in a private school with just girls so she could concentrate on finishing school and getting into a good college."

"What school did you put her in?"

"I don't see what that has to do with Melanie?"

"Melanie's giving you money to put your kid in private school so I'm sure she asked which one. I mean, you would figure she'd make the checks directly to the school, but she made them out to you. Why is that?"

"It's just what she did."

"Ms. Murphy, I checked and your daughter's records weren't sent to some fancy private school they were sent to McDaniel High School, which is the neighborhood public school where her father lives. So, I'll ask you again. What was the money for?"

"It was for Lily to go away, at least as far as Melanie knew. I asked her for the money to send Lily away. I figured she knew what was going on and would happily give it to me to send her away, but she said no. So I told her the truth, and she changed her mind."

"What was the truth?"

"That I thought my daughter was having an affair with an older married man."

"Was she?"

"Probably."

Yates could tell by her one-word answers that she was hiding something. Kate started fidgeting in her seat; she tried to act like it was from the cold but she was nervous, and the stare down from Yates wasn't helping.

"Kate, I get the feeling there's something that you aren't telling me."

Kate sat there, staring at Yates, unwilling to say anything else.

"The problem is with these cases the truth always comes out, eventually. If you have any information about Melanie or Jeff that we should know and we, find out about it later. Well, that wouldn't be good for you because that's obstruction of justice, it's a criminal offense."

She tried to control her tears but couldn't, Kate began to sob right there in front of Yates. She was not going to go to jail.

"Tell me, Kate, what happened to Melanie? She was your friend; she was helping your family, your daughter. What happened to Melanie?"

"I don't know what happened to her. That's the honest truth. The last conversation we had was about Jeff."

"What about Jeff?"

"My daughter Lily was having an affair with Jeff."

"Your daughter is a minor, why didn't you report it?"

"I know I should have, but I went to Melanie instead. I didn't want him to get in trouble. I figured if I just sent her away, it would be over with; he would go home to her, and Lily would go to her father's."

"Kate, I need to talk to Lily."

"No,"

"Why not?"

"I'm her mother, she's still underage, and I don't give you permission to talk to her."

"Did Jeff rape your daughter, Ms. Murphy?"

"Oh, God no. I'm done talking," Kate said standing up.

"Were you blackmailing Melanie?"

Kate gathered up her things and started toward the door, "I don't have to take this. I came here to help you find Melanie not to hear this filth."

"Kate, if you were blackmailing Jeff and Melanie and it turns out something happened to her, you will be arrested for obstruction of justice and possibly conspiracy. You might want to sit back down and clear up a few things."

"I'm not saying another word to you until I have a lawyer, and you stay away from my daughters."

Kate slammed the door behind her and almost took out Alvarez as she ran down the corridor and out of the Police Station. Alvarez popped his head into the conference room to see if Yates was still in there.

"You sure have a way of clearing the room."

Yates shook his head, "You won't believe this. Jeff was having an affair with Kate's daughter Lily."

"Get outta here? Isn't she like 15?"

"17."

Alvarez shook his head.

"Kate went to Melanie and told her she needed to pay to send her daughter away. From the way Kate told it, if you read between the lines it sounded like she was blackmailing Melanie."

Alvarez asked, "Do you think Melanie confronted Jeff about it?"

"She probably did. It's plausible that they could have argued, and something accidentally happened to her. Either way, I want permission to do surveillance on Jeff, see what he's doing."

"I'm fine with that."

Yates quickly typed up his request and dropped it off with Alvarez on his way out the door. He had his sights on Jeff, and he couldn't wait to arrest him and put this God awful case behind him.

30

Sunlight filtered in through the tiny basement window. Brie stretched and readied herself for yet another day. Ever since their first night spent together, each night had followed the same pattern. Their new routine began with dinner promptly at five, followed by sitcoms until nine. Brian and Brie sat together in his living room surrounded by the outdated furniture, holding hands. She would smile when he laughed and sometimes she would actually mean it.

For the first two days of her new found freedom, she sat there apprehensive, not knowing what to expect. Like clockwork, when the credits finally rolled on the last sitcom for the evening, he would take her hand and lead her upstairs to his bedroom, always locking the door behind him. She changed into whatever he laid out on the bed, usually a lace or satin nightgown and prepared herself for what was to come. Their first time surprised her; she expected that the day would eventually come, but he was so gentle with her that the experience left her feeling like she had just been with a new lover. Brie knew people would consider it rape but rape was violent, this was not. She might not have sought out his affections, but she was a willing participant, even if she did just lay there.

When they were finished, he would escort her back down to her room where Brie would spend the next day until he came home. No longer chained, she was able to get back to somewhat of a normal routine. Brie got out of bed, stretched and began doing what Yoga movements she could remember from her afternoon classes. Laying on the cold cement floor was uncomfortable but the freedom to do it was worth it. After about fifteen minutes of Yoga, Brie showered and dressed.

Every morning, she would walk over and check the doors in the hopes that Brian might have left it open. Today was the first day she found it unlocked. It might be a trap or a test; she thought reluctant to venture through the door. She opened it up a bit and listened. She heard nothing but silence. She started up the stairs to the top and saw the other door opened to the kitchen. She tried the knob; it was open as well. Slowly, she turned it. Brie listened to make sure he wasn't at home. Hearing nothing once again, she walked through and into the kitchen.

It was markedly bright; her eyes took a moment to adjust before she saw the note with her name on it laying on the counter.

Brie,

Good Morning Love! I hope you had a good night's rest. I was running late this morning and didn't have enough time to make your meals. Please help yourself to whatever you might want and I will try to get home early.

Love,

Brian

PS. I see you :)

The, "I see you" part was Brian's way of reminding her that he had cameras everywhere. She even assumed, he had them in the bathrooms she just didn't know where. Some of them were visible, over the kitchen cabinets, the hallways, and the stairs. The only place she wasn't sure of was his bedroom, and now that she was free to roam the house, she wanted to find out more about him. Admittedly, the first thought in her mind was to make a run for it. She walked over to the door, stopped in front of it, running her hands over the door knob she thought twice about turning. Just as she backed away, a voice startled her.

"Good choice, Brie. Now I know I can trust you."

Brian's voice came over the intercom by the front door loud and clear as if he were standing beside her. Brie looked around for the button to communicate.

"Just speak, I'll hear you. There's no need to push a button."

"I wasn't going to do anything."

"I know you weren't, I can see you."

Brie started, "I was just going to walk around a bit" when Brian interrupted her.

"That's fine; I have nothing to hide from you. Look, I have to go to a meeting so I won't be able to talk or hear you for a while, but I can still see you."

Brie said, "Okay" but received no response back.

Instead, she turned around and made her way back to the kitchen where she settled at the white Formica kitchen island with a bowl of Shredded Wheat. It was not the most glamourous breakfast she could have made for herself that morning, but it was comfort food. It reminded her of her grandmother, the only person in her family she could say without a doubt, cared for her. She wondered if she died, would she get to see her grandma again? There were days when she had no doubt she would survive and see her family again but for some reason, today was not one of those days.

As she rinsed her bowl out in the sink, Brie remembered her grandmother and how many times she watched her as a child do the same thing. She hadn't been this nostalgic in years. Maybe it was the circumstances that made her wish for the simple days she spent at her grandparent's house. Or perhaps, it was something else. Brie finally realized why she thought so much of her grandmother while she stood in the kitchen, it was her house. It wasn't exactly her house; the layout was a tad different, but the furniture was exactly as she remembered. The bowl dropped from her hand at the realization that she was living in a sort of replica of her grandmother's house. How this could be, she wondered aloud but had no answer. Brie turned the water off and ran into the living room and over to the two side chairs. She ran her hands along them. They looked exactly like her grandparent's chairs. She could see the picture from her mother's photo album that had her grandparents sitting in those same chairs holding hands. She looked at the picture a thousand times over the course of her life and could see it in her mind as easy as if she were holding it in her hand.

Brie went past the chairs and ventured up to the second floor. She didn't know if Brian was watching her and she didn't care. She figured that if Brian said they had no secrets from each other than he shouldn't care if she looked around. The first and second bedrooms were very plain with only just a bed and dresser, nothing remarkable about them. At the end of the hall was Brian's room. She looked around for cameras but saw none. She knew that just because she didn't see them, didn't mean they weren't there. She walked around carefully, waiting for the familiar voice to come over the intercom and tell her to leave. It never came, he either wasn't watching or he was telling the truth and didn't care what she found.

Brie started her search in his closet. She was about to dig into the two boxes on the floor when something shiny behind his shirt caught her eye. Brie pushed back the clothes to find a wall of pictures. Images of her and her children, as well as old pictures of her grandparents and her mother, covered the walls. The only person missing from the collage was Jeff; Brian had expertly cut him out of every picture and inserted himself. Some of them it was hard to tell that it was even a fake. Brie grabbed the photo from the day she brought Jack home from the hospital and shoved it down her shirt. She thought that if she ever got out of there, she would have a picture of Brian to show the Police. She repositioned the pictures on the wall so it wouldn't look like one was missing and moved on to the boxes. There were pictures of other women as well, other families that Brian had made himself a part of. Brie wondered if those women were missing too if they were dead. She took a few of those pictures as well to look at later, maybe she would recognize some of them, and secretly she hoped she wouldn't.

The old desk in the corner was covered in papers. Most of them were invoices for services rendered to The Greenly Corporation. The name sounded familiar to her, but she couldn't remember why. She quickly leafed through the stack until she saw a familiar email address, Jeff's. She wondered why Jeff would email Brian unless he'd been telling her the truth all along. She started to read them, inquiries about money transfers, Jeff going back and forth about when he was going to pay him and when they were going to meet. Nothing in the emails about what the money was for, but she could guess. Fifty thousand was a lot of money. The emails just confused her even more and didn't mesh with the pictures, the family he created in the closet. Brie wondered if she was just a job then why keep her? She assumed that they must have exchanged the money by now unless Jeff did want her dead and Brian didn't want to do it.

"Brie," Brian's voice called out from downstairs making her jump. Terrified, she tried to make everything look like it had before,

before jumping into the bed to pretend she was taking a nap.

When Brian entered the bedroom, Brie told him, "I was just resting."

"I figured I would surprise you and come home for lunch. I can work from home the rest of the day," he said as he leaned over and kissed her forehead. Before sitting beside her, Brian quickly scanned the room and noticed his closet door was slightly ajar. "I feel like now is the time to talk about things."

Brie sat up and crossed her legs before saying, "Okay."

"I know you've been looking around my room."

Brie attempted to interrupt him but Brian stopped her saying, "It's fine, we have no secrets. I don't want to you to be confused so I think we should talk, and I can explain what you've seen."

Brie nodded and waited for Brian to continue. He took a deep breath and paused like he was considering where to start, he reached out, taking her hand before he began, "The day we first met, I considered it fate. You didn't notice me. We just bumped into each other and went our separate ways, but you made an impression."

"Where did we meet?"

Brian looked away, "Where we met isn't important right now", he said as he got up off the bed and started to pace nervously, "The important part is that we did, you wouldn't remember that day anyway."

Brie sat very still watching him pace back and forth until finally he admitted, "I followed you home and I know that wasn't right, I mean, I'm not some freak who follows women. I just wanted to be near you. I watched you a lot. More importantly, I watched Jeff and I found out what he was doing to you and what he was going to do."

He paused, Brie felt like all the air had been sucked out of the room; her chest tightened, and her heart rate sped up.

Brian began again, "One night while I was in the woods behind your house, I saw Jeff. He was talking to someone on his phone, telling them that he would get a new phone soon and in the meantime just to email him. He didn't want to wait any longer; he was afraid he would lose his nerve."

Brian stopped pacing long enough to pull the desk chair around and sit backward with his arms crossed over the low back. He rested his head on his hands and started again, "I'm not proud of what I did, but I did it to protect you. Jeff had contacted a man named Mike Neill."

"That's Kate's cousin," Brie blurted out before she realized she had interrupted him, "He just got out of prison."

"I know. Jeff had planned to pay him to abduct you, maybe even kill you. He had canceled his plans when he realized that you had changed your will."

Brie sat there motionless; she remembered why she had changed her will, and she was glad she did; it had saved her life.

"So how did you get involved in this mess, Brian?"

He looked her in the eye and said, "I killed Mike Neill. I couldn't let them meet, so I killed him and took his place. As far as Jeff knows, I'm him."

"Why even take me then, if the whole plan was canceled?"

Brian knelt in front of her taking her hands in his, "Because I'm your family, and I've proven that I would do anything for you. You deserve a better man and I deserve my family."

Brie looked down at him; there were times where she felt like she was totally in control. Even though he had kept her locked up, chained and blindfolded, she held his heart in her hands. To him, that was more powerful than a gun and something she could exploit if she wanted to. She could no longer see clearly where the game ended, and the truth began. Brie attempted to run her fingers through his hair, but he grabbed her hands even tighter.

"Repeat after me Brie."

Brie nodded.

"Jeff is not a good man."

Brie mumbled, "Jeff is not a good man."

"I can't hear you, and I don't think you mean it."

Louder, Brie said, "Jeff is not a good man."

Brian kissed both of her hands before saying, "I saved you."

"You saved me."

"I love you."

"You love me."

He reached up and took her face in his hands and stared into her eyes before he continued, "I will always keep you safe."

"You will always keep me safe."

31

More than anything in the world, Jeff hated waiting. For years, he saw his ideas stolen at work until finally, he won his first Clio. The idea wasn't his best and now looking back he hated the entire campaign, but he was finally the success he always thought he should have been. Now, he was waiting for Laura to come out of school. Somehow he had to convince her not to talk to her parents and also calm her down. A nervous child is a loose lipped child but Laura was born nervous, Jeff thought, and now he would have to find a way to handle this one. He should have known better than to depend on her to keep a secret but he was in a bind, he needed to see Lily that night and Mike Neill. He never did get to see Mike.

This was the first and only time that semester that Jeff picked his children up from school. Jeff thought, it was a good thing he had a reason for being there. Otherwise, he figured it would look suspicious for him to linger around the high school. It wasn't much longer before they appeared, his daughter Jenny with Laura

walking behind her. They were both sulking about something when

Sara bounded up behind them and gave them a shove before

running off to her friends laughing.

Jeff yelled, "Girls," waving them over to him.

Sara immediately said goodbye to her friends, ran over and jumped

in the car, Jenny and Laura followed behind.

"What's got you so glum?"

Jenny responded for the both of them, "Nothing."

Laura quickly added, "I've got to go and catch my bus, Mr. Tate

before I miss it."

"No worries Laura; I'm giving you a ride."

Jenny hopped into the back seat of the Prius, but before Laura

could follow her, Jeff closed the door.

"I need to talk to you for one second, though."

Laura nodded.

"Jenny tells me you're upset, and I don't want you to be upset with me."

"I'm not upset Mr. Tate."

"I just wanted to clear the air, when I told you not to tell your parents, it's not because I did anything to my wife. I have no idea where she is. It was just, I needed a sitter for Jack, and I didn't want anyone to know because I was planning a surprise for Mrs. Tate. Now that everything has happened, if people knew you were at the house that night they'd think I did something wrong when I didn't."

Laura said sheepishly, "You could just tell them what your plan was."

"I can't do that Laura. They wouldn't believe me; I don't have any proof, and no one saw me. That's why you have to keep it a secret. If you don't want to do it for me, do it for Jenny, okay?"

"Okay, Mr. Tate. I will."

"Are we good?"

Laura looked down at the ground before mumbling, "We're good."

Jeff opened the car door for Laura so she could hop into the back seat with Jenny. He quickly checked his mirrors before pulling off in the direction of Laura's house. Yates waited a few minutes before following them. He may not have been close enough to hear what they were saying, but he was close enough to see the look on that child's face. He knew something was up, and he was going to find out what.

Laura Gardner lived at the very end of their neighborhood in what Jeff liked to call the McMansions. The house that he called home was a two bedroom shack in comparison. These homes were huge, more like estates. They had, at least, six bedrooms and a master suite that took up the entire back end of the house. It has to be 5,000 square feet, at least, Jeff thought as he pulled up in front of the house. Before bidding Laura a good evening, he paused to give her a quick wink and a smile to let her know that everything was perfectly normal before sending her on her way. The rest of the drive home, they sat in silence.

Yates parked down the street out of sight until Jeff pulled off and then after waiting a minute pulled in front of Laura's long driveway and walked up to the front door.

Laura's mother, Christina Gardner answered the door.

"Hello," Yates said extending his hand, "I'm Detective Stan Yates," he showed her his badge before he continued, "I work for the county police department, could I speak to you for a minute?"

"Christina Gardner," she said as she shook his hand. "Could you tell me what this is about first? My husband might want me to have a lawyer present."

"It regards the Tate family."

"Oh, that mess. I don't know all that much about them other than my daughter is friends with one of their girls. I don't know how I could help you."

"Ma'am, if I could just step inside. I'd prefer if your neighbors don't see me."

"Oh, yes of course," Christina said motioning him inside, "We can use this room over here."

She escorted him into a formal living room that was right off of the main entry way. A small room that made Yates instantly uncomfortable, everything was white. The only colors in the room save for the throw pillows, were the powder blue window treatments. It was the kind of room that a child never went into, impeccably kept and hardly used.

"Detective Yates, would you like something to drink?"

"I'm fine, thank you. I won't take up that much of your time. I wanted to know if it would be possible to speak to your daughter."

"Laura? Why would you need to speak to her?"

"I believe she might know something that could help the case."

"How?"

"Well, that's what I want to find out, Mrs. Gardner."

"It's fine as long as I can stay in the room with her."

"Perfect."

Christina excused herself to get Laura, who was upstairs in her room doing homework. Laura looked immediately terrified when her mother informed her that a Police officer was downstairs. She followed her mother, returning to the white room. Both Laura and Christina took a seat on the white Davenport sofa, both sitting exactly the same on the couch, backs straight, left leg crossed over the right with hands folded in their laps. There were mirror images of each other, dirty blondes with perfect posture. Yates could tell from the way she carried herself that Mrs. Gardner was not nouveau riche but instead, had probably had money her entire life.

"I've already explained to her why you're here, Detective."

"Well, then I'll be quick. Laura, I saw you today with Mr. Tate. Could you tell me what you both were talking about?"

Nervous, Laura responded, "He asked me about school... and he asked me if I told my parents."

Mrs. Gardner's expression changed to moderate concern when Yates held up a finger before she could respond. "What were you supposed to tell your parents?"

"He didn't want me to tell my parents; he said if I did they would call the police and he would get into trouble."

Yates was intrigued, what did this girl know. He urged her to continue even though he could tell she wanted to desperately keep her mouth shut. Tears were already starting to form in her eyes.

Laura stammered, "He didn't want me to tell... He didn't want me to tell anyone that I was babysitting Jack the night Mrs. Tate went missing."

Mrs. Gardner covered her mouth with her hands as she gasped, she could hardly believe what she was hearing. She knew without a doubt that her daughter was telling the truth, it was all over her face. The relief and fear that Laura expressed in her eyes told her everything she needed to know.

"Detective Yates, I think you need to leave. I need to call my husband and our lawyer before we talk any further."

"I understand but please I just need one more thing."

"Detective," Mrs. Gardner said more firmly as she stood at the entryway of the room.

"Laura, what time were you there?"

Laura looked at her mother who nodded her head that she should answer, "from around eight until about 9:30. He said he was only going to be thirty minutes, but he took longer."

Yates left the Gardner House pleased with himself. As soon as he got to the station, he was going to put in a call to the family's attorney to make arrangements to get a formal statement from Laura. Let's see you wiggle out of this one, you son of a bitch, Yates sang to himself as he got into his sedan and headed for home.

32

He knew he was taking a risk a meeting him, but Brian waited at the 7-11 just outside of Lorton anyway. No one was there this time of night even for its location right off of Route 1; that's why he picked it. That way, if anyone followed Jeff, there would be no hiding it. Across the highway there was an old abandoned motel, the windows boarded up, and weeds turned into mini bushes providing the perfect covering in the lot. He parked there and decided to walk across and wait on the curb on the left-hand side of the building that faced the highway and the back road.

The nights were already getting down in the low-40s, Brian hoped Jeff would be on time for a change. He didn't dress for the weather, just jeans, a tee shirt, and a black fleece hoodie. He would give him fifteen minutes, and if he didn't show up, he would text him that he got spooked and left. Brian had tried through texts to reassure Jeff that he didn't do anything and that if something had happened to Melanie, he had nothing to do with it.

Brian didn't have to wait long before he saw Jeff's familiar Prius pull into the parking lot. He waited a minute to make sure no one followed Jeff before he walked up to the vehicle and tapped on the glass.

Jeff jumped at the sound, "Jesus Christ dude, you scared the shit out of me."

Brian motioned for Jeff to get out and follow him. They walked through the parking lot and back behind the 7-11 finally coming to a stop at a secluded spot between two dumpsters.

"What's with all the cloak and dagger?"

Brian shook his head. To him, Jeff was the most annoying person on the planet. "I don't want to be seen by anyone talking to you; that's what's with all the cloak and dagger."

"I'll be real quick then, where did you take my wife?"

Brian laughed a little too loud then walked closer to Jeff forcing him to back up, "I didn't take your wife anywhere. I figured you just did it yourself to get out of paying me."

"No, not at all. That would defeat the whole purpose of getting the insurance money and going on with my life."

Jeff paused as if deep in thought for a second and then said, "I was wondering if you could do me a favor."

Brian stared at him but didn't respond. Jeff had a lot of nerve asking him to do anything as a favor.

"I was wondering if you knew a private investigator or maybe you could help me find out what happened to Melanie. Yates has it out for me, the Detective. He thinks I did it, and he's not looking at anyone else. If she's dead somewhere then I should know."

"Now all of the sudden you care. Two months ago you were hiring me to get rid of her."

It occurred to Jeff it was quite possible that Mike could be wearing a wire. He never once spoke in definite terms like that. He was always vague, at first, it was weird, but eventually, he got it and played along. This was the first time he had ever said aloud that he was planning to hire him to get rid of his wife.

"I never hired you to do anything, and we never talked about any harm coming to Melanie, so I don't know where you got that idea."

Brian realized he had spooked him, "I know, okay, calm down. I'm not wearing a wire. Jesus. The police don't even know we know each other, and I want to keep it that way. The further I am from this bullshit the better, I can't help you find out anything, and if you ask me, I think she ran off. Maybe Kate told her what you were up to."

"Kate wouldn't have said anything; she was getting half. She wanted that money more than I did."

"All I know is, I haven't said a thing and furthermore, I don't plan on saying anything so don't contact me again okay."

Brian left Jeff standing between the dumpsters as he made his way in the opposite direction of where he parked his car. He waited in the woods behind the 7-11 until Jeff left. After enough time had passed to ensure that no one had followed Jeff there, he walked backed over to his car and settled in for the hour drive back home.

He was in his own little world listening to the Delilah Show on the radio. It amazed him that there were so many people in the world

that just couldn't get this love thing right. To him, it was so easy;
he said to the radio, "you just love someone, and they love you
back, it's not that complicated." He wished they could hear his
advice as he listened to yet another complaint about unrequited
love. He was so into the show and making the necessary turns to
get home that he sped right past the library. He made a quick U-
Turn and doubled back so he could drop Brie's library books off in
the drop box. He kept meaning to drop them off, and they were
probably overdue by now. He quickly pulled them out of the trunk
and dropped them in the after-hours box before continuing home.

33

Yates sat in his office as he waited for Jeff and his lawyer, Mr.

Aaron Berkley. He didn't know much about him; he seemed like

he was just another average criminal attorney from what he could

find out. He could see Mr. Berkley waiting outside for his client to

show up. Jeff was now fifteen minutes late if nothing else you

would assume an attorney would stress to his client to be on time.

The phone rang, dragging Yates away from watching the scene

unfold outside. Alvarez just wanted to let him know he had

finished with Laura Gardner's statement and that he had emailed

him a copy. Just as he was about to sit down to read through it, one

of the officers knocked on his door to let him know they were

ready for him in Conference Room 1. Yates sent a copy to the

printer and grabbed it on the way to the room.

Mr. Berkley looked a lot younger close up than he did out in the parking lot. Yates thought about commenting on it but decided not to; the poor kid probably heard it all the time.

"Hello Detective Yates," Berkley said as he outstretched his hand. "I would like it noted that we're here willingly, but I would also like to note that my client feels like the department has been harassing him and we would like to say that this will be the last time we will acquiesce."

"Fine by me, let's get started then."

Yates opened up the brown expandable file he had with him and took out a stack of paper from a manila folder. "I'd like to go back to your original statement Jeff; I have some questions about it."

Jeff sat up straight from his previously slouched, I don't want to be here position. "We've gone over this like a million times. Nothing has changed, what questions could you possibly have?"

Berkley sat there taking notes, and Yates wondered what he could be scribbling down before saying, "I want to go back to the evening of October 2nd, the night your wife disappeared. What did you do that night?"

"It's just like I said. Melanie left to go to Wal-Mart. I was watching TV 'til I fell asleep. I woke up it was around 11."

"And you never left the house between the time Melanie left for Wal-Mart and when you woke up at 11 that night?"

"That's correct."

Berkley interjected, "Surely that's not what you called him down here for?"

Yates scratched his head as he watched Jeff. He was dressed in a pullover and jeans; his hair was a mess, and he looked like he hadn't had a good night's sleep in weeks. Yates thought, He has to know his chickens are coming home to roost before starting again, "No, it's not what I called him down here for. I wanted to let him know that we finally have a witness that can testify to Jeff's whereabouts on the night his wife disappeared. I have her statement right here," Yates said as he held up Laura's statement all the while watching Jeff's reaction. Jeff held his face completely still; he didn't want to give away the fact that he was scared to death.

"That's great," Berkley said finally looking up from his notepad, "Who is it?"

"Laura Gardner."

Jeff's expression fell, he knew exactly what Yates had in his hand even if his attorney didn't.

Yates continued looking Jeff directly in the eyes as he leaned across the table, "I'll ask you again, Jeff. Is there anything else you'd like to tell us about that night?"

Berkley stopped writing and looked at Jeff. He had surmised that he was clearly out of the loop. "Can you give us a minute, Detective?"

"Sure, I have all day," he said as he walked out of the room closing the door behind him.

Once Yates was out of the room, Berkley said, "Is there something I should know."

Jeff shook his head no.

"I can't help you if I don't know everything. I'm here to represent you whether you did it or not; I can't help you navigate this process if I'm out of the loop."

Jeff looked away and out of the small window that had an unobstructed view of the parking lot. The wind had picked up since they had arrived and leaves would occasionally hit the window making a very slight ticking sound. "I went out that night. Laura is a friend of my daughter, Jenny. I asked her if she could sit in the house while Jack was sleeping so I could go out."

"What did you do while you were out?"

"I met up with Lily and made a few calls while I waited for her to show up."

"Who is Lily?"

"She's the neighbor Kate's daughter."

"Isn't she a kid?"

"She's 18 now."

"Was she 17 then?

"Yes."

"Is there anything else I should know about Lily?"

"She's pregnant."

Berkley shook his head; if Yates had this information, then he had a motive.

"Berkeley let out a big sigh before asking, "Who did you call because I don't remember seeing any calls on your phone records for that night other than to Melanie?"

"I have a throwaway phone. I was trying to get in touch with this guy Mike Neill."

"Who's he?"

"Look, I don't feel comfortable talking about all this in here, can we do this in your office or something?"

Berkley got up, went to the door and motioned for Yates, who was waiting outside of his office, to come back into the room.

"So are we ready to finish up, gentlemen?"

Jeff shook his head yes and sat up again from his slouched position.

"I know you weren't home, so where were you?"

"I asked Laura to babysit for me so I could run an errand. I needed to meet a friend."

"This friend's name?"

"Lily Murphy."

"How long were you with her?"

"About an hour maybe two, I don't remember. I lost track of time when I was out with her, and I rushed back home. When I got home, Melanie wasn't there, and I just wanted to have a rest, so I laid on the couch and fell asleep."

"How long after Melanie left did you leave?"

"About twenty to thirty minutes. It took me awhile to get a hold of Laura."

"Okay, fair enough. I have another question for you. Do you know a man named Mike Neill?"

Jeff paused, he wasn't going to answer this question. He watched the face of his attorney as he waited to see if Jeff was going to answer.

Jeff finally said after appearing to think about it, "Not to my recollection." "Do you think he's the one who took my wife?"

"That's doubtful," Yates said as he took out some pictures from inside the manila folder on the table, "We found Mike Neill the same night your wife disappeared in a dumpster behind a 7-11 in Lorton. He had been dead for weeks."

Jeff's eyes got wide when he leaned over to look at the pictures. His mind was racing, he had just talked to him, and he couldn't have been dead for weeks. The pictures were gruesome, his clothes covered in dark dried blood and his throat had been sliced open nearly decapitating him. Jeff could feel his stomach turning over; he quickly excused himself to go to the restroom. He made it only as far as the first sink before he vomited and then dry heaved for what seemed like forever. He looked at himself in the mirror and watched as beads of sweat rolled down his face from his forehead. In his head he kept repeating, I'm going to go to prison.

34

It was pouring the morning Melanie walked up the path to Kate's house. It was that in between time of the year where summer gives way to fall, and Mother Nature isn't quite sure whether she wants to make the days cold or not. Jack was bundled up and resting on her hip as she walked up the steps to Kate, who was waiting at the door to let her in.

"We need to talk," Kate said and practically pushed Melanie into the house. "I don't know what to do."

Melanie sat on the couch in the living room and dug through her diaper bag as she watched Kate pace the room frantically. She pulled out Jack's blanket, a few toys and gently sat him on the floor to play, "What in the world is wrong?"

"It's Lily."

"I thought we agreed only a week ago that you were sending her away to school this fall?"

"We did. Now I'm not so sure we can."

Melanie waited, Kate could be very overdramatic. Melanie was certain whatever it was, it most certainly wasn't as mind blowing as she was making it out to be.

"Lily's pregnant."

Those two words in the same sentence took her breath away for a split second. At that moment she was shocked, angry, saddened, and a little bit ill. Then it hit her, the truth, loud and ringing in her head like the bells at church and she laughed.

Kate was shocked that her friend would find this all funny. "This is not at all funny Melanie. How can you laugh at a time like this? My daughter is pregnant with your husband's child."

Melanie tried to stifle her laughter but she couldn't. She started to gather up Jack's things when she said, "I really need to go. I have no idea what you're going to do about Lily, but I've helped enough."

Kate walked over to the entry and blocked her path. "Look, Mel, I'm going, to be frank with you. I need more money; Lily is going to need child support. If you think I'm going to force my daughter to abort my grandchild, you've got another thing coming."

"Then you need to find the father and ask him for child support because I'm not giving you another dime."

"I'll go to the cops; I'll press statutory rape charges against him."

Melanie stopped trying to leave and turned around to face Kate. She couldn't believe that at one point she considered this woman a friend. "If you want to go to the police, I'm not going to stop you, but I'm not going to pay you another dime."

"We just need to take care of this amongst ourselves like we planned, I'm just upset, my daughter is so young," Kate said back peddling, she knew she had gone too far. The last thing she wanted was for Melanie to dig her heels in, she could be incredibly stubborn.

Melanie thought carefully about the words she was about to say, she didn't want to say them out loud and especially not to Kate, but she knew that if this was going to go away, she had no choice. "There's no way Jeff is the father of Lily's baby."

"How would you know, they came to me and told me together. Jeff said the baby was his."

Melanie's face grew hot; she could feel her cheeks flush. It just galled her that this entire thing played out behind her back with her so-called best friend and her husband. It made her wonder what else they may have plotted. "I'm telling you, the baby is not Jeff's so if your daughter is pregnant then she got knocked up by someone else."

"Are you calling my daughter a slut?"

"No, I'm saying like mother like daughter."

It took everything Kate had within her not to strike Melanie, but she was holding Jack, so she restrained herself.

Melanie continued, "You have been throwing yourself at my family ever since your husband left you. Everyone in the neighborhood knows why he left you, hell even our realtor when we bought our house told me to keep an eye on you and to keep you away from my husband. I knew he could never be interested in trash like you, so I wasn't worried."

Kate interrupted, "Bottom line, my daughter is pregnant, and your husband is the father."

Melanie adjusted Jack to her other hip and said, "My husband can't get anyone pregnant. Why does everyone assume when you have IVF it's because there's something wrong with the woman."

"You have three children together Melanie; you can't expect..."

Melanie interrupted, "We have two children together, Jack is not his. He has a hormone imbalance; his sperm is bad. In fact, it was a miracle we were able to have the girls. When we went back to have the IVF for Jack, the doctors said he didn't produce enough to do it, so I just picked some sperm out of a catalog."

Kate completely floored, stammered, "Then why would Jeff say the baby is his?"

"He doesn't know. I know him, and he would never look at Jack the same way he does the girls if he knew Jack wasn't his. He would never have agreed to let me do it."

"He should know."

Melanie walked over to where Kate was standing. She was so close

Kate could feel her breath on her face. "If you tell him anything, it will be the end of our arrangement. You'll do what you planned Kate. Send Lily away and if she is pregnant, she can have her baby there. I'll send you what I already promised, but I'm not paying child support."

****

Lately, it seemed Brie hated to dream. Her old life with Jeff seemed nothing but a dim memory now. Each day away was another moment lost that she would never get back. The prospect of going home now seemed foreign to her. She would never return to the home she once had, even with all of its imperfections, it was still her life. Being with Brian had made her stronger. Being forced to live a life without Jeff had made her realize that she could.

It was colder than normal that morning in her basement room. Brian's side of the bed was still warm so it couldn't have been that long ago that he left for work. He had only allowed her to stay upstairs with him for that one night. Almost every night since, he visited her while she was sleeping only just to lie beside her and fall asleep himself. On the nights they had sex after he walked her back to her room, she could hear him pacing above. The sound of his footsteps beat out a rhythm that lulled her into a relaxed but usually haunted slumber.

Brie sat up maybe a little too quickly because the motion made her head spin. She closed her eyes tight and waited for the wave of nausea to pass. After a few minutes, she was able to move again, she splashed some cold water on her face from the bathroom sink and sipped a little from her cupped hands. The water was as cold as the cement floor beneath her feet, she was now ravenously hungry and not being able to hold out for the bowl of cereal that awaited her upstairs, she shoved the remnants of a half-eaten granola bar in her mouth. Chewing loudly, she walked upstairs only to find the door locked. She tried it again, yielding the same result.

"Brian," she shrieked almost frantic at the prospect of not having something more to eat. She banged on the door but no answer. Then she remembered, the door was old and sometimes it stuck, Brian had shown her that she had to pull the door towards herself and then twist the knob for it to open. After a few tries using that method, the door opened. Brie rushed into the kitchen and made herself a hearty breakfast of eggs, pancakes, and bacon. While it cooked, she enjoyed a bowl of Lucky Charms.

Brie passed the remainder of the day in the basement with very little interruption from Brian. There were times when she could tell he was watching her; she could feel his presence, almost tangible around her. She imagined him in his office, with his laptop open viewing her like she was a movie that only he could know the ending to. The sun had started to set before she heard the bell chime, Brian was home. Brie stood at the top of the stairs and watched as he put away the truckload of groceries he had spread across the kitchen island.

"Are you ready for Thanksgiving?"

Brie smiled and lowered her head before saying, "Yes."

"Wonderful. I have everything that we put on the list."

Brie looked at the groceries on the counter. She truly wanted to believe that Brian would keep to his word and she would be home for Christmas or at least reunited with her children. She was missing all of Jack's firsts. This would be his first Thanksgiving, and she would not be there. She wondered if Jeff was going to give the kids a good one. Brie tried not to think about it, but it was the only thing on Melanie's mind.

35

Mr. Berkley's office off Oronoco Street in Old Town comprised

the entire first floor of the renovated Victorian. Everything about it

was generic as if he reclaimed it from an 80's office movie set, lots

of browns and muted colors. Jeff sat in the waiting room listening

to Berkley's office manager Claudette whisper into the phone and

then pause to look over her horn-rimmed glasses at him. She

couldn't have been any older than Jeff, but it seemed that life had

not been kind to her.

"He'll be with you in a moment," she said quickly and returned to

her hushed phone call but not before giving him the stink eye. Jeff

could tell that Claudette was one of those "the darker the berry, the

sweeter the juice," type of Black woman. Throughout high school

and college, Jeff had dated anything with a vagina and had had an

80% success rate. He was quite proud of that fact and could say

unequivocally that it didn't matter if the berry was alabaster or midnight, it was all just as juicy.

Jeff rolled his eyes and went back to playing Candy Crush on his smartphone. He hated the fact that everyone assumed he was guilty. He was guilty of many things but killing his wife wasn't one of them.

Mr. Berkley finally came to the door of his office and ushered Jeff in to have a seat.

"Aaron, you're looking a little worse for wear yourself this morning," Jeff said trying to make a joke. It was an awkward situation, having to seek representation by a man you once went to college with, but he was the only one in their town who would take his case.

"It was a long night. I was up until almost dawn going over everything the District Attorney has for both cases."

"How does it look?"

"It looks bad, and honestly, I think the only reason you haven't been arrested is because they want a body. They have no proof that your wife is dead."

"It's because she isn't."

"Do you know that for a fact," Berkley asked as he rubbed at his temples. He should have never taken this case. His wife told him not to, begged him was more like it, but he needed the money and the publicity.

"No, I don't."

"Exactly."

Jeff was aggravated, he figured that if anyone should have his back, it should be Aaron but, by the way, he was acting, he could see the regret written all over his face. "Do you still want this case? I could find another lawyer if you don't want to do it?"

Berkley looked up from his notes and mumbled, "Yes," before going back to the stack to find what he was looking for. "So what do you know about Mike Neill?"

"I know him, but I can't tell the Police that because it will look bad."

"Yeah, it looks bad. The guy's dead and your wife is missing."

Jeff put his head in his hands before steeling himself and sitting upright again. "Look, I know this is going to sound crazy but, the guy they showed me, isn't Mike Neill. At least not the one I know. I mean, once I got past how nasty the pictures were, I could tell it wasn't him."

"The Medical Examiner identified him from his fingerprints; he'd been in jail."

Jeff interrupted, "I know all that, but I'm telling you, the guy I met was not that guy."

The lightbulb finally went off in his head, and Berkley jumped up, "I'm following you. You're saying that this guy you met with could be the one that has Melanie AND could have killed the real Neill?"

"I mean, it's possible. All I know is I didn't do it."

Berkley rummaged through another stack of papers and then yelled out to Claudette to get him a meeting with the District Attorney's office.

"I'll see what we can do on that front, maybe some sort of plea deal because you'll have to admit to conspiracy to even get them to believe this story you're telling me."

"I have the proof right here on my other phone," Jeff said pulling out an old style flip phone and showing it to him.

"That's good; we'll turn it over to evidence so don't lose it or delete anything off of it. Is there anything you should delete off of it?"

Jeff shook his head and looked out of the window; it was starting to snow again. "Nah, if I'm going, to be honest then I gotta be honest. The only thing on the phone is stuff from Lily and phone calls to her and calls to Neill and Kate... maybe, I'm not sure if Kate's number is on there or not. All I know is, I had better not go to jail for killing my wife when I didn't. I swear, I never paid anybody, the money is still right there in the account."

"It's still a conspiracy, Jeff."

Jeff sighed loudly and stuck the phone back in his pocket. He had a feeling he was going to go to jail regardless. He thought about running, but that would make him look even worse, no matter how tempting the thought.

"I'll set up a meeting, see what they say. Just cross your fingers",
Berkley said as he stood up and outstretched his hand to shake
Jeff's.

As Jeff left the office, he said a quick goodbye to Claudette whose
only response was to roll her eyes again in reply. He wanted to say,
"You know my wife is half Black" but he figured that wouldn't
make him look any better in her eyes. He sat in his car just staring
out into the lot. Tiny snowflakes covered the windshield of his
Prius. He wasn't ready to go back home just yet; he didn't want to
deal with all the family stuff for tomorrow. He didn't want to try to
salvage Thanksgiving when he knew it just wouldn't be the same
for them.

Their first Thanksgiving with the girls, they were almost a year old
and got into everything. Jeff remembered how easily Melanie
cooked a five-course meal and watched the girls while he watched
football. It was right out of a Norman Rockwell. Sometimes he
wondered where it all went wrong. When did he stop loving her
and start loathing her? It was all the small things, at first, the career
he didn't want, how easy everything came for her, the life he

wanted to have versus the one she wanted. Melanie always got

what she wanted. She wanted kids, the house, the life that she had,

and she was perfectly content. Jeff wondered, what about what he

wanted? She never thought, not once, to ever ask him if he was

happy, she always just assumed that as long as she was, he would

be. She was wrong.

The vibration from inside his jacket pocket startled him; it was

Sara. School had let out early, and no one was home. He texted

Sara that he was on his way and instructed her just to wait outside

the house, he wouldn't be much longer.

36

The tink, tink, tink of the ice as it hit the window awakened Brie from a rare and thankfully dreamless sleep. The basement room was like an ice box, but she was sweating. Brian had curled up beside her, arm around her waist, his face nestled in her hair. His warm breath on the back of her neck made her shiver and ache for his touch at the same time. There was some part of her, the Brie part that was falling in love with him. She couldn't help it; she felt a connection to him that went beyond everything she knew of right and wrong.

Slowly, Brie lifted his arm from her waist and walked into the bathroom. The floor was like ice, and she hurried across it to the fuzzy blue rug that covered the bathroom floor. While her feet were no longer cold, her stomach was another story. Considerably light headed, she reached out for the sink to keep her balance.

Turning on the faucet, she leaned over the sink and dry heaved enough to times to awaken Brian.

Even though the door was ajar, he stood outside to give her some privacy. Brian asked as he tapped lightly on the door, "Are you okay"?

Brie splashed some cold water on her face and sank onto the carpet, "I don't know. Maybe I've caught a bug or something."

Brian opened the door the rest of the way and sat down next to her on the floor. The bathroom was so small that he was barely in the room with her. He felt her forehead.

"You're not warm at all," he said as he pushed her hair out of her face. She leaned over the toilet thinking she was about to get sick again, but there was nothing.

"Why don't you get back to bed, I'll get you some ginger ale and some crackers."

Brian went upstairs to get Brie something to eat from the kitchen but by the time he returned she was already asleep. He sat the glass of soda and crackers by her bed and pulled the blue blanket up to her chest before returning upstairs to start prepping Thanksgiving dinner.

Almost every evening the first few weeks that Brie spent with Brian, her dreams were nothing but her family and Jeff. This afternoon was no exception, almost as quickly as her head hit the pillow she was back in her living room, sitting across from Jeff. Only, this time, she wasn't herself experiencing the dream, she was Brie watching Melanie relive a moment of their marriage.

Jeff looked every bit of contrite or, at least, gave the best allusion to it that he could muster up. He had come clean to Melanie in part because he no longer wanted their marriage. He was hoping that his big confession would result in Melanie throwing him out of the house. He wouldn't fight her for custody or visitation. He would do what he needed to do for their kids to save face but nothing more. She wanted this and their family, not him and he was hoping against hope that she would let him move on gracefully and with a nice settlement.

Jeff reached for her hand, and Melanie pulled it away, "For the longest time, I just felt guilty. I would watch you being the perfect wife and mother or, at least, try to be. I would just wonder why I couldn't just accept it. Why couldn't I be content?"

Brie watched as Melanie sat there absorbing every word, unmoving and every so often her eyes would shift to the baby monitor. She could hear the girls snoring lightly in their cribs upstairs. It was at that moment; she decided she didn't care what Jeff did. She wanted her family, and it would stay together despite him or to spite him.

"Jeff, I've always known. Did you think that when you left for six months that I would believe you spent that time alone? She waited for him to answer and when he didn't she continued, "I don't care, and I still don't."

"But you didn't..."

Melanie looked him in the face; she knew she would never get the entire truth out of him. The story she received was the version of the truth that he accepted. Jeff lived in a reality that he created. There was no truth, just a story, over time that became reality.

Melanie took his hand, "What I did or didn't do, doesn't matter.

It's not a competition."

****

Brian shook Brie awake. "Are you okay, you were moaning in your sleep?"

Brie rubbed her eyes; she was still a tad groggy, "I'm fine", was all she said before getting up to go to the bathroom. When she reentered, Brian was gone. The door at the top of the stairs ajar, allowing the faint scent of turkey and baked goods to drift downstairs. Brie slowly ascended staring into the kitchen when she reached the top. Brian was now donning a white and blue apron that was covered in flour and other food stains. He smiled at her and called her over to the table.

"Are we expecting anyone?" Brie knew the answer would be no, but she could hope. He promised her that she would be back with her family by Christmas. Hopefully, everything was going according to plan.

"Just us, that doesn't mean we can't have a feast. Everyone knows the best part of Thanksgiving are the leftovers."

Brie nodded her head in agreement. This felt all wrong to her, that little part of her that was still Melanie wanted to take one of the carving knives that was just within her reach and run him through with it. She could easily run away; he would be unable to chase her. Brie thought better of it; she knew she had nothing to go home to besides her children. Her friends weren't really her friends, and she had a husband trying to kill her. She was better off where she was or at least that was the lie she told herself. In enough time, that lie would become another truth.

"Dinner will be awhile, I started later than I wanted to but that's okay. I made some snacks and put them on a tray in the living room."

Brie excused herself and went into the living room. Brian had been busy in the overnight hours. She often heard him walking the floor at night; the stairs would creak as he paced. He had set up a table covered it with a fall tablecloth with a spread of different dips, veggies and chips. Brie wondered if it was homemade. From what she knew of Brian thus far, it was safe to assume that it was. Brie took a plate and scooped a few big helpings of what looked like onion dip and some carrots onto her plate. She settled into the armchair and began to zone out watching the football game Brian left on for her. It was then that she saw it, her picture flashed across the screen with a 1-800 number to call if you had any information that might help the police. Brie stared at the screen not knowing quite how to feel about seeing herself looking back. She turned her head to see Brian standing in the entryway, waiting for her response.

"Maybe we can put on a DVD," Brie asked?

"Good idea." Brian rummaged through the box that sat next to the TV and pulled out a copy of *It's A Wonderful Life*. "I was saving this for Christmas, but I guess we can watch it now."

Brian seemed to get very agitated when things didn't go according to plan, and the last thing Brie wanted was for anything to go wrong. Sometimes she felt as if her life depended on it. She nestled into the armchair drawing her legs up to her chest. Brian wrapped the blue and orange crocheted blanket around her shoulders before returning to the kitchen to check on dinner.

When the movie ended, Brie stretched and made her way to the kitchen, she stood in the entry and watched as Brian laid out everything perfectly on the table. He paused and looked up, feeling watched and when their eyes met he smiled. That moment was everything he ever wanted, if time could stop at that moment and he could live forever in it, he would be happy the rest of his days. But time marches on, making those tiny moments of exquisite happiness a fleeting memory that one strains to hold on to in their last days.

Brie ate quietly taking her cue from Brian. It was him who finally broke the silence.

"How do you like the meal?"

"It's very good; you're an excellent cook. How did you learn?"

"My mother mostly, she always wanted a daughter, instead, she got me. To say I turned out to be a disappointment would be an understatement."

"I'm sure she loved you anyway."

"I'm sure she did, but she's dead now so I'll never know."

"You don't have any other family?"

"Just you."

"But I'm not your family; I meant like blood relatives."

Brian stopped eating and put his fork beside his plate, "You may not be my family by blood, but you are family here", he said placing his hand over his heart, "and that is where it counts."

Brie smiled and continued to eat.

"A man has a child with a woman and automatically they are family, forever, bound by the life they created. You and I are no different."

Brie puzzled asked, "How do you figure that?"

"We are bound together Brie, forever by our shared circumstance. Nothing will ever break that bond; we are family and family is the most important thing."

37

Assistant District Attorney Lara Wilson took a seat at the table next to Detective Yates. It was the day after Thanksgiving, and neither one of them wanted to be there. Wilson didn't want to make any deals with Jeff Tate, but she was under orders to do so. The note from the library was proof of life as far as they were concerned and a happy resolution to this case was what her boss wanted. As they waited for Jeff and his attorney to join them in the conference room, she pulled her long braids back into a sophisticated ponytail. The change in hairstyle made her look less like Jenny from the block and more like she wouldn't take any shit from anyone and that's just how she wanted it.

Jeff walked around nervously in the parking lot behind the station; it had been almost thirteen years since his last cigarette and today he seriously wondered why he had ever quit in the first place. He longed for one and the sight of smoke coming out of some home's chimney off in the distance only made his cravings for it more palpable. He tugged at his hair a little in a vain attempt to relieve the stress of it all, and when that didn't work, he went back to pacing. Berkley pulled up a few minutes later in his slightly broken in black Honda Accord. Jeff extended his hand to shake his, and as they made their way to the station, Berkley gave him a very brief pat on the back to assure him everything would be fine.

The room was overly warm; it might have been freezing outside and threatening to snow at any moment, but the room made him feel like he was at a tropical retreat.

"Jeff," Lara said extending her hand, "I'm the Assistant District Attorney Lara Wilson. We're going to record this interview", she paused and looked at Berkley before continuing, "Today is Friday, November 27, 2015. Present are Jeffrey Tate, his counsel Mr. Aaron Berkley, Detective Stanley Yates and myself Assistant District Attorney Lara Wilson."

Jeff swallowed hard and fidgeted in his seat. The chairs were hard and uncomfortable; he imagined that anyone subjected to sitting in these chairs for more than an hour might confess to anything just to get out of there. It was unbearably hot, and he had already removed his wool coat and sweatshirt revealing a tee shirt that read, "Guns Don't Kill People, Cops Do." It was inappropriate, and when he put it on, he thought nothing of it since he had the sweatshirt. He was running late that morning and pulled the only clean tee shirt he had out of the ever-growing mound of laundry.

"We have a note here we'd like you to look at and tell us if you think it looks like your wife's handwriting," Yates slid the plastic-wrapped piece of paper across the table to Jeff.

As Jeff read the words, his heart leaped out of his chest for just a moment and then sank, "Yes, it is her writing, where did you get this?"

"It was found by a librarian a few days ago. We tried to trace where it came from by who last checked the book out but it was listed under Mike Neill. As you know, Mr. Neill is deceased. We were hoping you could shed some light on this," Wilson asked looking at Berkley waiting for him to say something.

"I don't know anything about it."

Yates put the note back into his box of evidence. Now that the murder of Mike Neill and Melanie Tate's kidnapping were linked, the amount of people working on this case doubled in size overnight.

"I thought we were here to talk about a deal you had for my client," Berkley said, irritated.

"Yes, we are," Wilson said sizing up Jeff. She then continued, "Based on the information initially provided to us by Mr. Berkley about what we can expect to hear from your testimony here today the District Attorney is prepared to negotiate on lesser charges if the information provided leads to finding Melanie Tate or an arrest."

"That's not what we discussed," Berkley interrupted.

"I understand, but you also have to understand that your client is not only admitting to conspiracy to commit murder but also statutory rape…"

Jeff interrupted, "I never raped anyone."

Berkley told his client to be quiet before focusing back on Ms. Wilson, "I understand the need your office might have to get my client on something, but I cannot counsel my client to take this offer."

"I'll be right back," Lara said before she stepped out of the room to pretend to call the District Attorney. She had hoped her plan to get the information without a concrete offer would work, but she underestimated Berkley's savviness because of his messy and at times downright slovenly appearance. She waited a few minutes before reentering and said, "We won't charge him with conspiracy but the other charges will be dependent on the investigation."

Jeff nodded his head, the least of his worries was the rape charge. He knew Lily would never say that he raped her. The last thing he wanted was to go to jail for something he didn't do or for something he did.

"Let's start at the beginning Jeff," Yates said, "When did you first meet Mike Neill?"

"It was the middle of September, we texted each other and emailed but mostly texted. We met at the 7-11 in Lorton off of Route 1."

"Why did you meet with him?"

"I needed access to my wife's money; Kate was blackmailing me because I got her daughter pregnant. She said she would go to the police unless I paid her $250,000. I didn't have that kind of money, but my wife did. I had tried multiples times just to get her to give me access, but I think she knew something was up, and she took me completely out of her will and off all the accounts. She gave me $50,000 which I put into a savings account."

"Berkley said you have a phone in your possession that you're going to turn over that proves all of this?"

Jeff handed Yates the burner phone and watched him drop it into the bag before saying, "Note for the record, Jeff Tate has handed over into evidence one black Samsung flip phone."

Wilson sat there taking notes along with Berkley as Jeff continued, "When I got the money I planned to give it to Kate, just to shut her up. When I tried to give it to her, she didn't want it; she said she had a better idea, and it involved her cousin Mike. She said Mike could get rid of her for me and then I could have access to everything and take care of her daughter. I didn't want to kill my wife, but I did want a divorce, and Melanie wasn't going to do that, ever. I told her fine, but I wanted no parts of it, I would give him the money, and that was all. When we had our first meeting, I chickened out and told him I didn't want to do it anymore, and I would deal with Kate on my own. It was a quick meeting."

Yates pulled out a mug shot of Neill, "Did the guy look like this?"

"No, this guy's hair was much lighter, and the face was totally different."

"If we gave you some pictures to look at, do you think you could pick him out?"

Yates pulled out two large binders of pictures and sat them in front of Jeff before he and Lara left the room and walked down to his office.

"We need to bring Kate Murphy in," Lara said as she closed the door to Yates' office.

****

"I've looked through these books for two hours, he's not here," Jeff said as he closed the last book exasperated.

Berkley went to the door and motioned down the hall for Yates to reenter.

"Any luck?"

"No," Jeff said feeling spent, "What now?"

"Kate is in the next room; we're going to interrogate her based on the information you've provided us."

"Am I free to go?"

"Sure, you're not under arrest, you came in of your free will. We'd like it if you'd stay just in case we have any follow-up questions. If you'd like some lunch, we can have some brought in."

"Thanks," Berkley said before his client could say anything, "We'd appreciate that."

"I'm going to go and smoke," Jeff said as he walked out to the parking lot, as he left he looked over into the other interrogation room hoping to get a glimpse of Kate. He couldn't see her; all the blinds were drawn. He stood outside, leaning against the wall just killing time. They didn't know he didn't smoke anymore; he just wanted to get away from it all. For the first time since this entire ordeal began, he felt sorry for Melanie. What had he gotten her into?

38

The bedroom was cold, Brian leaned over and kissed a sleeping Brie on the cheek before getting out of bed to turn up the thermostat. He returned a few minutes later with a glass of water and sat it on the nightstand. Laying back in bed with his arm around Brie, sleep found him a lot quicker than it normally would have. Normally, he drank anything with a proof before bed. It ensured he wouldn't dream; he hated to dream because he couldn't control what his subconscious mind desired to fixate upon. Tonight, it would be Beth. No amount of alcohol could ever blot her out entirely.

****

Brian sat on the bed anxiously awaiting Beth's arrival back at the house. The doctor had already called him with the news. He was preparing a celebratory gift for her return; they were going to have a baby, and he couldn't be happier. When Beth walked into their bedroom, he could tell in an instant looking at her face that she was not happy.

"I just heard the news," Brian said embracing her, "I'm so happy."

"We need to talk."

"Okay."

"I want a divorce."

"What are you talking about, we haven't even been married a year yet. Beth, whatever it is, whatever I've done wrong. I can fix it."

"You can't fix it," she said as she pushed past him and into the walk-in closet where she started to grab her clothes and shove them in a bag. "I'm tired of living this fake ass life with you."

"It's not a fake life baby; I love you. Can't you see that?"

"You don't love me, you love, love. You want a family; you want the shit you see on TV, and that's all fake."

"That's not true baby," he said stopping her long enough to put his hand on her stomach, "This is what we created."

"We didn't create anything. This baby isn't even yours. Do the math, stupid. We haven't fucked in six months if it was yours, I'd be showing by now."

The wind knocked out of him; he watched as she continued to pack her things saying nothing. He saw the gift box laying on the bed, beside it the scissors he had just finished using to curl the pink and blue ribbons. He thought about the tiny onesie inside it and the baby that would never wear it. Heat flooded his body, and he escaped to the master bath to cool himself off. Looking at himself in the mirror, he watched as tears streaked down his face and it disgusted him. He mumbled to the man to the reflection looking back at him, "I can't believe I'm crying over that whore." He splashed water on his face; she would never see him cry.

He walked out of the bathroom a different person, he was full of animosity and vengeance when he grabbed her by the arm and dragged her over to the bed, bending her over it. She tried to shove him away, but he was much stronger. Grabbing her by the hair with his left hand, he used his right to lift up her yellow dress and tear off her underwear.

Beth yelled, "Stop", and clawed at the bed trying to pull herself away. The sheets crumbled in clumps under her hands.

Brian growled, "You always liked it rough," as he continued to take her from behind he told her calmly, "Just shut up." He hated her so much, so much that he would do something like this. Then he looked over at the scissors; he could see himself picking them up; he wished he had the courage just to slit her throat at the moment and be done with her. He twisted her long brown hair around his left hand and yanked on it as he climaxed. He had pulled so hard that when he finally released her hair, some had come out in clumps in his hand. He laid relaxed on her back, panting. Her hair clung to his face mixed in with sweat. It was then that he saw it, the blood, pouring out of her neck, the scissors dripping, still in his hand.

Brian awoke with a start, he sat straight up in bed panting, sweat pouring off him.

Brie asked politely, "Are you okay?"

"I'm fine. Just a stupid dream," He said, and then he kissed her on the lips. "Go back to sleep."

Brie did as instructed as she listened to Brian's footsteps cross the floor to the door and faintly trail off down the hall. Brian went downstairs to find his backpack he carried every day to work. It was sitting on the floor beside the entryway table. He knelt down and began to rifle through it until he found what he was looking for, a small oak memory box. He ran his fingers across the smooth polished wood as he lifted it to his nose. As he inhaled the woody aroma he closed his eyes, his body relaxed but not enough, he would have to complete his ritual. He went to the green armchair and turned on the table lamp before sitting down.

With the tiny box resting on his lap, he opened it. Inside lay five small envelopes, each a different color. He picked up the yellow one labeled Beth and opened it. Out of it, he pulled a length of her hair tied with the pink and blue ribbon. It still felt hard as he rubbed it against his face not soft like the other ones. Delicately, he placed Beth's hair back into the envelope, and he ran his fingers over the others trying to decide which one to do next. He skipped over the white one that he had yet to label with Brie's name and picked the blue one labeled "Jane". The long strand of blond hair uncurled in front of him; this one was his favorite, it was so soft and smelled like peonies, just like she did. He often wondered how it kept its smell, but he always knew Jane was special.

The sun was starting to come up, tiny flickers of it began to pierce the white blinds of the front windows. Brian put Jane's hair back into her envelope and smelled the box one last time before putting it away and returning to bed.

39

Kate sat in the conference room waiting impatiently for someone to enter. She knew Jeff was there somewhere; they drove past his car in the parking lot. She wondered what he could have told them. Kate knew that Jeff would sell out his mother to keep himself out of trouble, so it was safe to assume that he told them everything and left out all the bits that made him look bad. Yates strolled into the room with a small packet in his hand and held it out to Kate.

"What's this," she asked reading the warrant but not quite understanding it?

"It's a copy of the warrant currently being executed in your house. A judge has granted me the right to search your property, your phone records, and your bank accounts."

"Am I being arrested?"

"No, not yet anyway. While we're here waiting, let's have a conversation."

"About?"

"How about the truth, Kate? You and Jeff have been blowing smoke up my ass for weeks and meanwhile a woman has been missing."

Kate sat there looking Yates in the eye but not saying a word.

"Jeff already told us about Lily and your attempt at blackmail. He even told us about your cousin Mike."

"So if you know everything, then what do you need me for?"

"Because there are two sides to every story and I think you deserve to tell your side. If you don't, with the story that Jeff is painting if we find anything that corroborates his version of the truth, we'll arrest you. You're facing possible conspiracy charges, murder if we don't find Melanie alive, extortion, corruption of a minor, should I keep going?"

Kate hung her head and stared at the brown Hermes bag sitting on the floor next to her chair. It was the same bag Lily stole from

Melanie's closet a year ago. Kate had every intention of giving back when she found it but instead decided to keep it. Now with Melanie gone she could use it without fear of anyone knowing. For as much as Kate loved Melanie, she hated her. She looked at Melanie's perfect husband and family, their life of never having to want for anything and she hated her for it. The day she caught her daughter kissing Jeff was the best day of Kate's life, it was then she knew that Melanie wasn't perfect either.

"Have you ever been tired of your life, Detective Yates?"

Yates nodded his head in agreement.

"My whole life, I've been last. Last child, last in my class, I barely graduated. Then I fell for a man who didn't love me; I was his last choice as well. So I settled, and I wound up a forty-three-year-old divorcee with two kids and a house I can't afford but can't afford to lose", Kate sobbed and rubbed the tears that were forming in the corners of her green eyes. She was every bit of sad and angry flipping between wanting to punch a hole in the wall and curling up to cower in the corner. "When I saw a chance to better my situation, I took it. Opportunities don't come knocking for women like me; I have to make them."

"You saw Melanie as an opportunity?"

"I saw her piece of shit husband as an opportunity. It never occurred to me that what he was doing was wrong. My girl is old enough to make her own decisions, hell I was fourteen when I started having sex with men who should have known better, that's just how life goes Detective. I went to Melanie and at first, she didn't care, she knew her husband would never leave her because he liked the money. When Lily came up pregnant, I had proof of the affair and would do a paternity test to prove it. She didn't want that."

"Why not?"

"She knew that Lily's baby wasn't Jeff's."

Yates looked at Kate puzzled and asked, "How?"

"Melanie had to use a sperm donor to conceive Jack. Her IVF wasn't taking with Jeff's sperm, and she was scared that he would tell her enough was enough, so she used a donor through the hospital."

"Does Jeff know?"

"I doubt it, why else would she agree to pay me to keep my mouth shut about it."

"What do you think Jeff would do if he found out about it?"

"If that's your way of asking me if he'd kill her, no, he wouldn't. He'd leave because he never wanted all those kids anyway. If anything, she would have killed him before she'd ever let him leave. When Melanie said, 'til death do us part', she meant it literally."

"If you knew that Jeff wasn't the father of Lily's baby then why would you go along with the plan, why not just cut your losses and walk away?"

"Jeff is an idiot. He'd never even think for a moment that the child wasn't his. It could come out looking Black, and he'd still say it was his. He wants out of his marriage. He thought if he confessed to Melanie that he got someone else pregnant, she'd finally give him his walking papers. But like I said, Melanie said death do us part, and she meant it."

"But why kill her?"

"As far as I know, he didn't. I don't believe he ever would. My cousin Mike said he could make it look like she was abducted and killed. Melanie only had provisions in place for her life insurance policies, but Jeff had an accidental death policy on her. The policy covered death by homicide. Mike was supposed to keep her until the policy paid out, then when we all got our cut, Jeff would disappear, and Mike would release Melanie."

Yates scribbled more notes down on his pad before excusing himself to go to his office. He reviewed his notes with the woman standing beside him whom Kate could just barely see. She watched as the Wilson shook her head and walked away. When Yates finally came back into the office and said the words she had been waiting to hear, it was almost a relief to finally hear them; she could stop worrying about the when because that time had now come.

"Kate Murphy, you have the right to remain silent..."

40

The hot water slid down Brie's body as she stood in the shower. Although she was eating well, she could tell she had lost at least fifteen pounds if not more in the two months she'd spent with Brian. It felt good to relax and let down her guard, something she was only able to do while he was at work. As she stood there, chin touching her chest, eyes closed breathing in the steam her thoughts trailed away to her home.

She could never go back. She knew it wouldn't be the same; she had slept with another man. Brie mumbled to herself, "You don't want Jeff anymore anyway. I should want him; Melanie loves her husband and her family". It was like to she had to remind herself and saying it aloud made it true but it was only half true. Melanie stopped loving her husband after the first time he cheated on her, but if she were really going, to be honest with herself, it was the first lie. The first act of betrayal, over something stupid she didn't even remember anymore. That was when she loved him a little less than she did the day before and over time it just eroded away. They became business partners, and their company was their family, the image they portrayed to their neighbors. At that, they flourished but something was always lacking, devotion. That was what she found in Brian, no matter how insane it was, he was devoted to her. Melanie could never accept Brian but Brie could.

The lights went out in the bathroom and soon after the water started to go cold. Brie turned off the shower and dried off. Shivering, she rushed for her robe and quickly tied the belt around her waist. The power was out; she could hear the tinkling of the ice as it hit the basement window. It took a few moments for her to realize what was happening and that Brian wasn't watching, he couldn't see what she was doing, she could leave.

She quickly threw off her robe and pulled on some warm clothes. She had no coat, but there was a sweatshirt with a hood, and if she wore layers, she might be warm enough. Melanie looked around for shoes, but she had none. Going up to his room there were sneakers but way too big for her feet, she wouldn't get very far in them, and she needed to move quickly. She had no idea where she was or how long it would take to get help. Melanie put on two pairs of socks and then her slippers and ran toward the front door. She double checked again to make sure the power was still out and reached out her hand to turn the knob.

The voice in her head that was Brie said, "Don't do it. If you leave, you can never come back. You'll never see Brian again. He'll go to jail or worse, do you want that on your conscience?"

She was panting now, she didn't know what to do, and the walls felt like they were closing in on her. She took her frustration out on herself, balling her hands into fists so tight that her nails dug into her palms drawing blood. She stared at them, crying silently at her open palms, watching the red lines trace a trail down to the floor. Melanie sat there on the bottom step, unable to fight Brie and mentally broken down, she wept.

****

"The weather is getting really bad out there, Brian. Maybe we could put in a request to close up shop early," Laura asked silently hoping the request was already made.

Brian had been oblivious to the storm outside his office window; he had been on the phone most of the morning dealing with a security breach. It was of his creation, but his manager didn't need to know that. In light of the breach, his manager gave him the administrative rights he had wanted all along. They didn't care what he did, just as long as he fixed it.

"I'll handle it," was all he said before closing the door in her face. He grabbed his phone off the side table and stared out the window thinking that the ice would be beautiful if it weren't such a damn pain in the ass. It would take him forever to get home now. The storm had completely covered his car in ice; it would take him at least thirty minutes to get it off. He looked down at his phone and pushed the black box app to check in on Brie. Nothing happened. The screen was completely dark. Nervous, he went to his desk and tried to log into the program, but that didn't work either. He had to get home; it would only be a matter of time before they came for him. He closed his laptop, not bothering to shut it down, grabbed his backpack then yelled down the hall to Laura, "Close up, I have to run out."

The roads were a mess; Brian only bothered to scrape the ice off the driver's side windows, and now he was regretting that decision, everything looked distorted and hazy. His frustration only grew by the time he entered the highway, no matter which lane he entered, the top speed never past 25mph. He felt like he would never get home and then finally, forty-five minutes after he started, his neighborhood came into view. He drove slowly down the street looking everywhere for the slightest clue that anything was wrong. Seeing nothing out of the ordinary, he ventured to pull into his driveway.

"She's gone, I know she is," he said to himself when he went to open his front door. Surprised to find it still locked, he opened it only to be relieved to find Brie sitting at the bottom of the stairs.

"I didn't mean to do it," she said still crying.

Brian dropped his bag and kneeled down beside her, "It's okay."

Brie collapsed into his arms and wept, "I couldn't leave you."

Brian brushed the strands of hair away that had fallen on her face.

That's when he noticed the streaks of dried blood on her face.

"What did you do?"

Brie continued to cry and repeatedly say, "I tried, but I couldn't leave, I'm sorry," to the point where Brian could no longer discern whether she was apologizing to him or herself. As he checked her wrists he saw the source of the blood, large bloody welts raised and inflamed on her arms as well as her palms where the initial wounds had dried and formed soft scabs. He sat with her on the floor just holding her, this fragile little thing that was unraveling like a frayed bit of yarn in his arms. They laid there together, half sitting, half laying on the bottom step just staring into each other's eyes saying nothing, there was nothing left to say.

41

Brian loved getting up every morning, going through the ritual of getting dressed, making breakfast, and kissing Brie goodbye. Even on a day like today, a rainy and cold first of December, his insides were warm and filled with all that gooey heartwarming stuff portrayed on the Hallmark channel. He wished it could stay like this forever, his little universe but their time together would draw to a close soon enough; he could feel it in his bones. It was time to move on, and Brie had to go.

Maxine tapped on his office door before making her way to the office and sitting in a nearby chair. Brian looked up from his monitor only briefly enough to acknowledge her presence.

"Christopher wants to know if you've finished with the database upgrade," she asked before running her fingers through her hair and fluffing it to make it look fuller.

"I have. Once it upgrades tonight, everything will be as it should be," Brian said quickly hoping she would leave, but she stayed. "You know, you could have just IM'd me that question, there wasn't a need for you to walk all the way down here to my office."

"I'm trying to beat my friend," she said holding up her wrist and showing off her hot pink Fitbit, "she beat me last week, there's no way she's winning this time."

Brian half smiled at her and thought, "The dimwitted get caught up in such trivial pursuits," before saying "Well, even if you don't win at least you're exercising."

Maxine looked at him like he had no idea what he was talking about and mumbled an, "I guess" before picking out all of the red M&Ms from the bowl on his desk and popping them one by one into her mouth.

Slightly annoyed that she was still lingering in his office, Brian asked her, "Can I help you?"

Maxine looked like the cat that had swallowed the canary; she was bursting, to say something but Brian could tell she wasn't quite sure if she should.

"What is it, Maxine?"

"Well you know I'm kind of hanging out with Darryl right?"

"No, I don't keep tabs on your love life."

"Oh," she said sounding a little disappointed, "Well, anyways, he told me that you have made deposits downstairs. Is that true?" Her eyes were big waiting on him to confirm or deny.

"Yeah, I have, so what of it."

"Did they pay you?"

"No, I did it for free. I'm an employee; they can't pay me for it."

Maxine got out of her chair and walked over to the desk to pat Brian on the shoulder, "That is just so great, I mean you're helping people. I mean, because of you someone will have the family they always wanted."

"Family is the most important thing, Maxine. That's why I do it."

"But you don't even have one of your own yet, and you're helping others."

"It's fine. It's no big deal. Now, if you don't mind. I have to finish up some things if this update is going to happen tonight."

"Sorry," Maxine said hanging her head as she slinked out of his office.

"Oh Maxine," Brian called before she could leave, "Can you keep that between us, it's supposed to be anonymous."

"Oh yeah, no problem," she said before closing the door behind her.

Now more than ever, Brian was glad to have full access to the database. It would only take a few keystrokes before he would be able to go in and erase any trace of the fact that he had donated sperm to the clinic. He was pretty sure that no one would ever connect the two but even if they did, he would have the insurance of knowing that he deleted all of the records.

It didn't take long before he found his donation file marked Anonymous #A329450. The donations were only anonymous to the woman getting the donation. The company could always go back in their records and find out who exactly it came from. That was the record he had to find and delete. It took another five minutes, but he found it, Brian Kirby, #A329450. He deleted the record and tagged it as a duplicate entry. He smiled when the expected error came across his screen and asked if he was sure he wanted to delete the connection between this record and record #R231872. He clicked the OK button and watched the blue bar fill up to reflect the deletion process.

When the process was completed, he went back into recipient record #R231872 to double check. As far as the records were concerned Melanie Tate was a patient of the clinic and that was all. Once the update occurred that evening, it would permanently delete all records of Brian Kirby.

What in the world is he doing here, Brian thought as he watched from his office out of the corner of his eye as Maxine escorted Detective Yates down the hall to the other conference room. There were times that having an open office plan came in handy, what it lacked in privacy it made up for in warning. Brian looked over at his backpack and for a moment, he let his nervousness overcome him. It was only a moment, just long enough for him to break a slight sweat before telling himself that it could not be for him.

"Brian, there's a Detective Yates in the conference room. I can't find Christopher, could you talk to him?" Maxine asked her best begging face.

"Where's Chris?"

"I think he left early for that meeting."

"What does he want?"

"Access to records he said, he has a warrant."

"Then have someone in Legal talk to him."

"Ray from Legal brought him up here; he said it was okay to give him the information he requested. I just don't know how to pull it."

Exasperated, Brian said, "Fine," and got up from his desk.

There were exactly forty-five steps between Brian's office and the second conference room, thirty-five to the elevator. At the thirty-fifth step he took, he debated whether he should go to the elevators to leave or keep walking, he decided to keep walking. Outside the glass doors, Brian took a deep breath before opening them with such authority that the one on the right stuck in place and caused him to miss a step upon entering.

"Detective," Brian said as he extended his hand, "I'm Brian Kirby, how can I assist you?

"Hello. I have a warrant for any information you have on file for Melanie Tate including donor information.

"Of course, if you wouldn't mind just waiting here, I'll run back to my desk and print it out for you."

As Yates watched, Brian when to an empty cubicle and logged in to the database, printed out Melanie's file and double checked it once again to make sure that he would not come up. He didn't. On his way back into the conference room, Brian heard Yates on his cell phone talking to someone. He paused outside the door where he could hear but not be seen.

"As soon as he's finished with the composite, send it out like I said. If you can, get someone to email it to me because I won't be back to the station for a while, I'm following up on Kate Murphy's statement." There was a pause where he listened and then said, "I'm at the clinic now." It was then that he noticed Brian standing behind the door, and something clicked from his memory. He knew this guy; somewhere he'd come across him, and he just had to jog his memory.

Brian handed Yates the records in a manila folder and asked if there was anything else he needed because he had to attend a meeting.

"No. This will do. Thank you," Yates said as he got up to follow Brian back to the elevators. "You know, you look familiar to me. Have we met before?"

"I doubt it."

"I never forget a face, and it's been bothering me, especially when I just saw you standing there. I got the worst feeling of Déjà vu."

"I wish I could help you. That feeling is annoying like you're playing cat and mouse with your memories."

Yates walked into the elevator, once the doors closed. Brian returned to his office. He couldn't take any more chances; his time was drawing to a close. He went to his laptop and executed his script that would take him completely out of the employee database. He wiped down his phone, keyboard, and desk. He grabbed his bag and waited for the elevators.

In the parking lot, Yates was about to step into his car when he received the email from Alvarez. He opened the attachment to see Brian's face staring back at him.

"Holy shit!"

Yates threw the papers into the front seat of his car and started to run back toward the building. He had dialed Alvarez and could hear the call ringing in his ear as he ran.

"The guy from the picture, he's here in the clinic," Yates puffed out.

"Huh?"

Yates banged on the elevator button several times in the hopes that it would come quicker.

"The guy from the sketch, I just talked to him, he works here at the clinic. I need back up."

Yates dropped the phone back in his pocket and got onto the elevator. The elevator would get him there faster than trying to run up ten flights of stairs. He bounded off the elevator and went straight back to Brian's office despite Maxine's attempts to stop him. Yates stood outside his empty office; he now remembered where he last saw him from. Brian was the guy from the trail, the one looking for his cat.

"Where is he?"

Maxine worried that something was terribly wrong stammered, "You just missed him, he's gone home for the day."

42

"I need you to get downstairs, Now!"

"Well, hello to you too," Brie said not understanding why Brian was so gruff.

"I'm serious. Downstairs."

She got up as ordered and watched him run upstairs out of the corner of her eye. Brie sat down on her bed in the basement, waiting. She could hear the pounding of his footsteps on the stairs above her. She listened as her pulse quickened with each trip he made up and down them. By the time he reached her, he was a sweaty mess. She said nothing as she watched him go over to the radiator and bring the chain out again.

"Why?"

"You've done nothing wrong. The Police are coming to rescue you, and I don't want them to think you had anything to do with this. I need to shackle you again."

Brie did not put up a fight. She understood his reasoning, even if she did hate the chain. She was excited and terrified at the same time; she was going home.

"I need you to take these," Brian said handing her two small pills.

Brie stared at the tiny white pills he placed in her hand afraid to take them but knowing she had to do as he said. She trusted him, even though he gut told her that she shouldn't.

"They're painkillers and a little old so one might not put you to sleep. I need them to think I held you here and kept you drugged. When they find you, they'll run all sorts of tests and find the drugs in your system. You'll just fall asleep, I promise."

Brie obliged and took the pills.

"Are you leaving right now?"

"No, we still have some time. Just lay still. I'll be right back."

He was gone for a while before he returned, so long that Brie had fallen asleep waiting. Trying not to wake her, he slid into the bed beside her. Brian watched as the late afternoon sun came in through the tiny window illuminating all the little specs of dust as they floated around the room. Brian thought about all the beauty there was in little things like that. He curled up on the bed next to Brie, holding her in his arms and for just a few moments, he let sleep find him as well. Brie was very warm, her heart beat, a lullaby that sang him to sleep. He did not want to give this up, but he knew he had to.

When he woke up the room was dark, but she was still asleep in his arms. Brian slowly shifted and very gently so has not to wake her, kissed her lips. Turning, he grabbed the long hunting knife he left on the nightstand when he came back down and found her sleeping. With one hand held her head, with the other, he ran the blade across her throat. He could feel the warmth of her running through his hands. He held her close and sobbed into her hair inhaling her scent hoping to take every bit of her essence with him.

He stayed with her the rest of the night. He had more than enough time; the police would follow his breadcrumbs as he had laid them out. There was no doubt in his mind that Detective Yates went back to the clinic only to discover that his employee file erased.

His manager, Christopher would run the query and eventually stumble across the deleted file, but that would take at least two days maybe one if the Police department did it themselves. That address would lead them straight to his house where they would find Melanie. At some point, when they ran his social it would come up that Brian Sayers died at the age of 10, some twenty years ago in Florida. Keeping his real identity safely concealed.

Brian lifted Melanie from the bed and laid her gently on the floor as he changed the sheets. When he finished, he repositioned her on the bed and set about cleaning the house from floor to ceiling. He wasn't worried about them getting his DNA, they already had that anyway from the clinic, he just hated to leave a dirty house. In the shower, he put the finishing touches on his new hair color, a dark brown. He threw away his contact lenses and went back to his horn-rimmed glasses; he preferred those anyway. He gave the house one last once over before closing the door and getting into his car to leave for good.

Brian sat in the driver's seat for a few minutes; he hated goodbyes, but the clock was winding down. He turned the key in the ignition and drove toward the highway, throwing Brian Sayers' passport and driver's license out of the window. The *Hawaiian Christmas Song* playing on the radio prompted him to veer left and pull onto the I95 ramp going south. He would drive until he grew tired and then hopefully fate would provide him with a sign of where he should stop. With his new identity, waiting for him in the glovebox along with enough cash to live under the radar for years, he could go anywhere.

43

Brian watched as the evening news anchor said, "It's been six months and investigators are no closer to finding the man that abducted and murdered Melanie Tate. You'll remember the discovery of her body in the basement of a house in Glendale. Residents are now petitioning the Mayor to have it torn down, citing everything from decreased property values to attracting a criminal element to the once quiet neighborhood. The State and Local police have requested we once again share this man's photo. They believe he is not only responsible for the abduction but also may have a connection to other unsolved disappearances and murders. If you've seen this man, please call…"

Brian closed the window before the report could finish. Reduced to a blurb, no news is good news, he supposed. As he sat at his desk, he received an alert on his phone that his sperm was used. Every time he received one of these alerts he got excited. To him, the family was the only thing that mattered. This time, he would be smarter, he would take this one while she was still pregnant. It would be too difficult to get them all after they were born. He could admit his mistakes; everything has a learning curve. Now that Detective Yates was on to him, he was glad that he gave his final donations under a pseudonym. This place didn't use pictures, just descriptions. His description fit everything that a woman wanted in a donor; his stats made him perfect.

He stared at the name on his screen, Christina Baker. She was 38 years old, unmarried but she had a good job and could take care of a child on her own. She looked a lot like Beth if Beth would have aged to thirty-eight. She's perfect; he thought as he dug a little deeper into the file and got her address before logging out. He had learned a lot about women from Brie; he would put that knowledge to good use. "This will be the last one," he promised to no one in particular.

It was a gorgeous summer day, just how he liked them. Warm with a just a slight breeze was the way to go. If only every day could be like this, then life would be perfect, he thought. He had had perfection once and lost it. Never again, he had a foolproof plan. He went through everything in his mind as he waited for the top of his Mustang convertible to fold down. It was an old car, but he liked old things, old things lasted.

The open road loomed before him empty, as he cruised down the highway, he flipped on the radio, *Somebody to Love* by Queen was playing, he turned it up louder and sang along. He would try again, he thought as he plugged her address into the GPS, having a family was the only thing that mattered, it was the most important thing.

ABOUT THE AUTHOR

M. E. Matthews is a graduate of The George Washington University and alum of the Yale Writer's Conference. Her writing has been featured on Scary Mommy, Huffington Post, Mamapedia, and BlogHer. You can also find her writing in the anthologies; *Motherhood: May Cause Drowsiness* and *Surviving Mental Illness Through Humor*. When she's not writing for her blog Scattered Wrecks she's on Instagram looking at all the pretty pictures and taking a few of her own. Michelle lives in Northern Virginia with her husband, daughter, twin sons, and Meepers the cat.

ACKNOWLEDGMENTS

I wanted to write something witty and heartfelt, but as I stared at my laptop screen, the only thing I could think of was a simple "thank you."

Sometimes the most important thing is to express simply how you feel as succinctly as possible. Of all the people in this world, I would like to thank for helping me get this novel out of my head and onto the page, I would be remiss if I didn't start with my husband, David. Brian and Melanie would still be the playmates of my daydreams if David didn't push me to the keyboard.

Secondly, I would like to thank my family, friends, and Beta readers. The lines between all three of those have often blurred, and I am so grateful to have everyone of you in my life. Your support of me and of my ability to put words on a page that people would even want to read has often astonished and humbled me.

Last and most definitely not least, I would like to thank you for spending your hard earned cash on my words, I hope they entertain you.